AT A MOMENT'S NOTICE

A Witness to Murder

CAROLE ALEXANDER

Inspired by true life events!

Copyright © 2015, 2025 Carole Alexander.

All rights reserved. No part of this book may be reproduced, stored, or transmitted by any means—whether auditory, graphic, mechanical, or electronic—without written permission of both publisher and author, except in the case of brief excerpts used in critical articles and reviews. Unauthorized reproduction of any part of this work is illegal and is punishable by law.

ISBN: 979-8-89419-632-9 (sc)
ISBN: 979-8-89419-633-6 (hc)
ISBN: 979-8-89419-634-3 (e)

Because of the dynamic nature of the Internet, any web addresses or links contained in this book may have changed since publication and may no longer be valid. The views expressed in this work are solely those of the author and do not necessarily reflect the views of the publisher, and the publisher hereby disclaims any responsibility for them.

One Galleria Blvd., Suite 1900, Metairie, LA 70001
(504) 702-6708

Dedication

This book is dedicated to the father that I never knew. True life events overwhelmed him and he left our family under truly mysterious circumstances. Never heard from again, his absence had a profound effect on all of us.

Acknowledgements

Special thanks to Ann McIndoo, my Author's Coach, who got this book out of my head and into my hands.

My most grateful thanks to Keith Delavin, my Literary Agent, who has consistently encouraged me and assisted me in the promotions of this book.

Contents

Chapter 1	Susan's Funeral	1
Chapter 2	That Fateful Night	6
Chapter 3	Raging Bull	9
Chapter 4	Where is He?	13
Chapter 5	First on the Scene	18
Chapter 6	Jonathan Seeks Refuge	22
Chapter 7	Angelo Runs for It	25
Chapter 8	The Police Begin to Search	30
Chapter 9	Shattered Dreams	34
Chapter 10	On the Run	38
Chapter 11	Officer Bandeau is Full of Surprises	42
Chapter 12	Angelo's Capture	47
Chapter 13	Taking Stock	51
Chapter 14	Timing is Everything	54
Chapter 15	Plan B	57
Chapter 16	Tommy's Wrath	60
Chapter 17	In the Woods	64
Chapter 18	A New Resolve	67

Chapter 19	Eddie Looks for the Patellis	71
Chapter 20	More Hidden Problems	75
Chapter 21	Tommy's Business	78
Chapter 22	NYPD Case Status	82
Chapter 23	Resistance	85
Chapter 24	Protection	89
Chapter 25	The Big Fancy House	93
Chapter 26	The Road to Change	97
Chapter 27	Jennifer, Where Are You?	100
Chapter 28	The Worst Kind of Death	104
Chapter 29	Priorities	108
Chapter 30	Failure	113
Chapter 31	Case Closed	117
Chapter 32	No Resistance	120
Chapter 33	Richard Bandeau Returns to NYC	123
Chapter 34	We're Going Home!	126
Chapter 35	Who is Missing?	129
Chapter 36	Jennifer's Next Step	132
Chapter 37	Viola	135

Epilogue: One Year Later 139
About the Author 143

CHAPTER ONE

Susan's Funeral

Although it was a lovely summer day in August, Amanda was in tears. She and her siblings had buried their mother, Susan Anthony, earlier this morning. She was now seated around a table at Carmine's Times Square Italian Restaurant with some close family members and friends reminiscing about Susan and sharing memories about family events.

Wiping tears from her face, Amanda looked at her older sister Michelle, who asked her, "Amanda, tell us what you found out about Daddy. Now that mom is gone, I think it's ok to know what happened. We would finally like to know the truth. Will you tell us?"

Mom was always so tight-lipped about what happened so many years ago, she referred to it as "daddy's disappearance". Amanda thought about it for a few moments, looking at all the expectant faces around the table. With a deep sigh, she decided it would be okay to relax over a meal together and share the intriguing family history she had learned about recently.

And so Amanda begins the story of her family, beginning with how their parents, Jonathan and Susan, met when she was just fourteen years old, and Jonathan was eighteen. Susan was a budding beauty, and Jonathan was smitten with her from the very first moment he saw her. They met at a park near her home, being introduced by his friend, Thomas, who knew her brother. He courted her in the proper fashion, taking his time, eventually asking her father for her hand in marriage when the time was right. He was determined to make her his own from the first time he had held her hand.

Over time, the two became inseparable friends, going to the movies, frequenting their favorite nightspots on the weekends, and always had Sunday dinner at her home. During Susan's summer vacations from high school they enjoyed picnics in the park, watching the animals at the Bronx Zoo, going to Coney Island and swimming at the beach. It was a long and romantic courtship.

Now here he was, handsome as ever, standing next to her, marrying her after seven long years of waiting. She looked beautiful. The wedding of Jonathan and Susan Anthony on March 26, 1938 was quite a social event.

They had a church wedding at the Holy Name of Mary Catholic church in Valley Stream, New York. Two hundred and fifty guests crowded into the beautiful church to witness their marriage. After the groom kissed the bride, they followed the happy couple to the reception at the groom's spacious family home where there was a five-piece band waiting to welcome the newly wedded couple and their guests to the celebration. There was so much food! The wait staff kept refilling the buffet with platters of delicious foods favored by each side of the family.

Jonathan's family was German-Italian and they favored specialty pastas, bratwurst and sauerkraut, pirogues, rib roast stuffed with apples and prunes, and a potato stew with dumplings. Susan's family was Norwegian and favored all kinds of fish and shellfish, plus potato lefse, chicken fricassee, Arctic Grub, and pinne-kjott. No one went home hungry!

There was an open bar providing refreshments and lots of festive dancing in the glassed in sunroom. The band played a wide mix of music from the 1920's and 1930's, including such favorites as "Stardust", "Putting on the Ritz", "The Way You Look Tonight", "I'm in the Mood for Love", and "Smoke Gets in Your Eyes". The couple looked into each other's eyes and Jonathan held his new bride close to him as they danced and swayed to the romantic music.

The young couple left the reception early amid cheers and laughter. They had planned a short honeymoon at Niagara Falls, NY, before settling down in their new Manhattan apartment. They had a wonderful time and Susan returned from Niagara Falls with stars in her eyes, absolutely certain that she had married the right man.

Jonathan worked as a parking garage manager on West 151st Street, and Susan worked for Chase Manhattan Bank as a secretary. They were enjoying their newlywed status, learning how to live together as a married couple and trying to become pregnant.

Jonathan and Susan planned to build a home in the country where they could raise their children in a safe and clean environment. They spent time on weekends scouting around for a perfect location for their country home. After several months of searching, they found two possible locations on Long Island, each piece of property approximately four acres in size.

Just a year later, in 1939, World War II began and Jonathan was called into action by the Armed Forces. He was to serve in the Philippines for the next four years. During this time Susan chose the property for them on Long Island as well as secured the location while prices were low and while waiting for her young husband to return.

They planned to build their own home on Long Island before Jonathan returned to his former employer.

Early in 1944, Jonathan returned home from the war, and when springtime arrived, he began working on their country home. He did still enjoy life in Manhattan with his young bride, and they were still trying for a family. After what seemed an eternity, and no baby, the young couple decided to adopt a child. Her name was Michelle. Michelle was such a blessing and they loved being parents. To their surprise a few months later, the couple conceived and their daughter, Jennifer, was born in 1947.

Jonathan was not overly ambitious in his work efforts on the house on Long Island, and in 1947 the house was still not finished. Impatient with the length of time it was taking to finish the house, Susan decided it was time for her to take some action. She packed up the kids and moved out of the Manhattan apartment to occupy the unfinished house.

Arriving at the house unannounced really surprised her husband, but Susan also got a surprise – a very unpleasant one. Jonathan was not done with the house because instead of working on the house he had been entertaining some of the local ladies! Now he was caught red-handed in bed with a young woman named Beatrice. Beatrice couldn't get out of the house fast enough, leaving Jonathan to deal with the consequences.

Susan had known about his infidelities after the war. She knew there was a woman in California, as that woman was brazen enough to have called the house a couple of times asking for Jonathan. Susan had also intercepted letters and photos from California, depicting many of Jonathan's infidelities. It was so painful to be confronted with this truth, but Susan had ignored this, thinking he would straighten up and fly right once he was a family man again, and busy working on their dream home.

After a night of thinking about the situation, Susan confronted Jonathan and told him what they were going to do. He would now return to his job in Manhattan and work on the house during his days off. She and the children would live in the house on Long Island, and she would continue to work on the house during the day when she was not busy with the children.

Yes, it would slow down the progress of completing the house, but she felt in control of the situation and that was the best solution she could think of.

The entire group at Carmines had been listening intently as they had never heard any part of this story before. They could not believe their ears as they learned of Susan's deeply hidden secrets and painful heartbreak.

Susan never let on how deeply pained she must have been. What an amazing woman! Michelle burst out, "Yes, yes, Amanda. Get to the story of what happened to Daddy! We all want to know what Mommy told you near the end. We want to know the truth that she would never tell us!"

CHAPTER TWO

That Fateful Night

It was Tuesday, March 5, 1957, and it was her birthday, Candice Pratel had turned thirty two. She and her husband, Shelby, went into New York City that night to celebrate her special day. They left home around three in the afternoon and drove into Manhattan, parking in the same parking garage they always used on trips into the city. Located near the theater district at 140 W. 51st Street, they parked their 1955 two-tone blue Chevy Bel-Air Convertible on the lowest level.

That particular evening the weather was just perfect! The skies were clear, the air was crisp, and it was about forty-five degrees. The Pratel's spent the evening dining out at Sardi's, located on West 44th Street. This was a rare treat for them because of their limited budget. As pastor of a small church, Shelby often needed to work a part-time job as well, but tonight he was treating his beloved wife to a special evening

For dinner they enjoyed a sumptuous meal of rack of lamb, complete with all the trimmings. They even indulged in a bottle of champagne - Shelby was toasting his beautiful Candice again and again. After dinner they attended the opening show of Carousel on

Broadway. It was such fun to see Barbara Cook playing the role of Julie, David Atkinson as Billy, and Ruth Kobart as Nettie.

What a great time they had! Walking back to the garage, they were laughing and joking around, singing songs from the play, their favorites were "You'll Never Walk Alone" and "What's the Use of Wonderin'". They were not paying too much attention to their surroundings and they had not quite reached their parking spot when out of the shadows lunged a short, stocky, dark-haired man right in front of them. He immediately began firing rounds into the young couple. Caught by surprise, there was no time to scream or protect themselves. Both Candice and Shelby were dead before they hit the cold cement floor.

The hired gun was Angelo Comino who had been sent by mafia boss Tommy Two Toes Carudente to kill the couple who had testified against him in court.

The couple who had testified against Tommy Two Toes were Samuel and Carolyn Patelli. They lived in the same Northport, New York village, had the same initials, and Shelby even worked occasionally for the same employer as Samuel.

This was a case of mistaken identity. Angelo had gunned down the wrong couple!

When Tommy Two Toes found out the Pratel's had been killed, and not the Patelli's, he went ballistic with rage. And to complicate matters even further, there was a witness to the Pratel murders. The parking garage manager on duty that night, Jonathan Anthony, had seen the whole thing.

Jonathan had been walking to his car when he saw Angelo charging out of the darkness with a pistol in his hand. Scared that he would be seen, Jonathan quickly stopped in his tracks and hid behind a car, watching as the cold-blooded killer shot the couple, checked for a pulse and finding none, calmly pocketed the gun and walked away. Jonathan had been holding his breath during this unbelievable scene, and now he let out an audible gasp, which Angelo heard.

The killer spun around and seeing Jonathan began chasing after him. As the killer chased after Jonathan, the killer began firing at Jonathan, who jumped into his nearby pickup truck and took off like a madman. Jonathan was fortunate to escape both the bullets and the killer, but now he was fearful and unsure of what to do.

As he was driving around the city, all kinds of questions were running through his head. Should he report to the local police precinct? Should he just go home and pretend he never saw it? Would that endanger his family? Would this hit man be waiting for him at work the next day? Should he just run away? He had so many questions circling around in his head, but no answers.

CHAPTER THREE

Raging Bull

Taking a sip of water and a deep breath, Amanda continues telling the family story to the group. It is actually a relief to finally be free to tell the truth. Now that her mother had passed away, her mother could no longer be hurt by it.

The thug known as Tommy Two Toes Carudente, was from the Bronx and was a well-known Mafia Boss governing several metropolitan boroughs of New York City, plus all of Long Island. Tommy Two Toes was brutal and ruthless, killing anyone who opposed his leadership or got in his way. Tommy was raised under torturous methods by criminal parents who were mob members, learning first-hand that obedience must be immediate and complete. His first and only error under the former Boss, Fingers Magee, rendered him with the absence of three toes when he was caught skimming $100 from the nightly boxing wagers – hence the name Tommy Two Toes.

Tommy Two Toes knew the importance of having his trusted right-hand-man around whenever a job is to be completed. He knew what could happen if you did not have an assistant who can witness and corroborate. After all, that is how Tommy came into the position of Boss - Magee did everything in private and there was no one to help him when Tommy came calling after the toes incident.

With no witness, who was to dispute Tommy's tale of what went down? Tommy came through the ranks violently, and so he gained his current position when he found Fingers alone at his office one night and Tommy shot him dead without even muttering a word.

Fast Eddy was always close to Tommy, standing at the ready for whatever his boss needed, with steadfast loyalty. Eddy was the perfect right-hand-man who learned his boss's preferences and obeyed immediately.

Angelo made the worst possible mistake, and still did not realize it as he stood before Tommy to deliver his report. His report included the fact that there was a witness - a witness that would be murdered upon arrival at work the next day. This was his first time working for Tommy and Angelo wanted to impress his new boss. Unfortunately, his assignment did not go perfectly.

Angelo is speaking with confidence, ignorant that the wrong couple was killed. "I can handle it Boss, no problem. I will be at the garage when the man arrives. I know what he drives and where he parks. No problem, Boss. I will not let you down". Suddenly there is an explosion of rage coming from Tommy, who is barely able to breathe.

"You incompetent fuck! You killed the wrong couple *and* you allowed a witness to escape! How can you stand there, claiming the job done with just a snag?" Tommy picked up a large machete that he always kept on his desk and began pacing back and forth in his large office. He began swinging the machete with razor sharp edges that glistened and flashed in the light, slashing the air into ribbons with a terrifying force. This machete destroyed everything it touched.

"*No problem,*" Tommy sneered. "*I can handle it.* You fucking idiot! I should finish you right here and now! You *will* take care of that witness tonight, and report back to me immediately. Got that? Now get out of here!"

Angelo quickly backed out of Tommy's office as he continued to rage like a bull, swinging the machete left and right. Angelo was terrified that Tommy's intent was to chop him up! He didn't turn around until Fast Eddy had slammed the door in his face, then he bolted out of there.

Finally out of Tommy's sight, Angelo was able to breathe a little bit and began to think about what had just happened. He had no idea he had screwed up so badly. He had killed the wrong couple! Shit! As he exited the building Angelo was sweating profusely, his hands were trembling and he was having difficulty breathing. He was terrified to think what Tommy would do to him if he didn't fix this, fast. Tommy had a reputation for quick and brutally harsh strikes against anyone who wronged him or made mistakes.

Although he was relieved to escape Tommy's wrath, and the machete, *he had to find a place to hide!* Angelo had lost all his bravado and he was petrified of Tommy Two Toes.

Tommy turns to Fast Eddy, who was standing in the shadows of the room.

"Eddy, see that the job gets done. I want the Patelli's hit to be finished; find that stupid eyewitness and make him disappear, too. Take care of Angelo. Make sure Angelo suffers a long time before he dies. And clean up this damn mess."

It is the end of a long day and Tommy wants to unwind at home with his lovely young wife, Lucinda, but he better blow off some steam before he goes home. He decides to spend some time at the gym, working out his frustrations as he pounded on the punching bag. He will beat the shit out of that bag until he calms down. As Tommy exits his office, he is muttering and cursing under his breath, still furious about the botched job.

Lucinda does not deserve his wrath; she is the only person on earth that he cares about. Although he's still furious about the mess Angelo made, he slowly begins to calm down as he thinks about his lovely Lucinda. "If anybody ever lays a hand on her, there'll be no place to hide" he thinks to himself. "I will hunt them down…" he mutters, as he heads toward the gym with a sinister smile on his face.

CHAPTER FOUR

Where is He?

A s Amanda told them the story, her listeners were fascinated. Other than an occasional sip from their drink, they were perfectly still, entranced with the story.

The night of the Pratel's murder, Daddy did not come home. Susan had made dinner and when Jonathan did not show up, she fed the kids and put them to bed. She waited up for him past midnight; she could not sleep. She lay there most of the night, tossing and turning, wondering where he was.

It was now four o'clock in the morning and Jonathan had still not come home. He was long overdue for returning home from work. "Where *is* he?" she asked herself. "I guess he is out with another girlfriend," Susan thought to herself. "Why do I put up with him? I wish he would settle down and be a real husband to me. I am so disappointed with the way my life is turning out - *we had such great dreams.*"

Jonathan was always a handsome sort; a real lady-killer. He was very charming and women seemed to flock to him naturally. Not only was he handsome and charming, he really cared about people; he had a kind word for everyone. Unfortunately for Susan, he did enjoy the intimate company of a female, even if it was not his wife.

Although she didn't share this with anyone until recently, Susan had experienced the pain and heartbreak of his interest in other women many times. Ever since they had met, there was always someone else in the background. She had fallen in love with him when she was fourteen years old and understood a man had certain needs, but she had naively thought that she would be his only one after they married. She wasn't. There were other women, sometimes more than one at the same time. Susan knew about his escapades with a woman named Viola when he returned to California from serving in the Philippines. Indeed, that would still be going on except she lives 3,000 miles away. But Susan had developed a blind eye to details of the recent occasions because it was too painful for her to bear. In her mind she knew what was going on each time Jonathan failed to come home from work, but her heart was unable to accept the truth.

She finally gave up trying to sleep and got ready for what she knew would be a very long day. Although she would have liked to stay in bed and wallow in self-pity, she talked herself into moving forward. It was the only way.

"If I get my day started I will feel better. I can focus on each job and forget about feeling bad. At the end of the day I will have enjoyed my children, gained another step forward in finishing this house, and stand proud that I am a strong-willed woman who takes no challenge sitting down." She kept repeating this to herself, still wondering what could have happened to Jonathan.

By seven that morning, Susan had been pretty busy and accomplished quite a bit. She had taken care of the chickens, picked up around the house, and organized the tools and materials for putting up the sheetrock in the living room. It was time to get the kids up, make breakfast and get them ready for school. Michelle was twelve years old, Jennifer was eight, and Amanda was almost three years old.

Susan and the kids ate their customary breakfast of oatmeal and orange juice, chatting about the day's upcoming events. The kids assumed that dad was asleep as usual, and Susan didn't tell them any different. After they had finished, they cleaned up the dishes, gave their mom a kiss and a hug and off to school they went. Susan watched as they walked down the long dirt driveway, laughing and giggling.

School was across the street for the two oldest ones, and Amanda would stay home with Susan, trying not to get underfoot as Susan continued to work on household projects. Her goal for that day was to have the living room complete with sheetrock and spackling, ready to paint the next day. She was quite the worker; Jonathan did not realize how lucky he was.

The work on the house was going slowly, working by herself on most days, but this was her dream – *their dream* - to have a home in the country to raise the kids in a good neighborhood and safe surroundings. Well, she had the kids – and for the hundredth time that day, she wondered, where *was* that husband of hers? It is now three in the afternoon, the kids will be home from school any minute, and Jonathan was still not home.

This is so typical of him; sometimes he would disappear for days with another woman. "I am tired of making excuses to the children. They miss their daddy so much when he is not around. Just last weekend Jonathan and Jennifer were cruising around the countryside in his treasured Willys Jeep, a 1952 military edition, laughing and giggling, having a tremendous time. He can be such a good father when he is around - *what can I do to change things?*"

As Susan pondered that question, she began feeling drowsy – probably from worrying about Jonathan.

"As soon as Michelle and Jennifer are home from school I will tell them to go do their homework; Amanda can stay with Michelle, and I will take a little nap before dinner." Around five o'clock, Michelle began preparing dinner. They were having Pasta Fagioli, Jonathan's favorite, and the kids were starting to ask questions: "Where is Daddy tonight? Is he working another night in the city? Why doesn't he come home at night like other fathers?" Jennifer asks.

Michelle is squirming in her seat as she states, "The kids in my class are beginning to laugh at me because Daddy is gone so much, so I made up a story about him being a traveling salesman. It's better than being made fun of. Besides, I like telling stories. I can make them happy ones instead of telling the real truth. I don't like it when Daddy's not around."

And with that, Michelle burst into tears. "It is not fair," she wailed. "I want a real daddy!" Now Susan was crying, and she hugged all three of them close to her. "I know, I know. He'll be home soon".

Later on when they are all in bed, Susan was having yet another sleepless night.

Susan was thinking about the effect Jonathan's absence had on the kids. They had now been married 19 years and he continued to be an inconsistent father figure for the children, leaving me alone for greater lengths of time as each year passed. It had been nineteen years of a rocky marriage, simply because he would not stay home.

When Jonathan was home, things were great. We didn't fight much, he seemed to love all of the children. He certainly enjoyed playing with them - he was like a kid himself. Why can't I entice him to come home after work each night? What could I do to make things more appealing here at home? *What will become of us if he cannot become a stable father? There must be an answer - and I am going to find it!* With that thought in her head, Susan finally fell asleep, well past midnight.

CHAPTER FIVE

First on the Scene

Officer Richard Bandeau had just started his uniformed foot patrol shift at midnight on March 6, 1957, when he heard gunfire shots echoing in the neighborhood shattering the dead silence of the night. He immediately ran towards the three-story parking garage structure, guessing intuitively that was where the shots came from.

As he entered the garage, it was dark and now strangely quiet. He pulled out his service revolver and proceeded silently into the building, unprepared for the horrific scene he found on the ground floor, just past the entry booth. There were two dead bodies, a man and a woman, lying next to each other on the floor, there was blood everywhere and there was no sign of the killer. *"What happened here?"* he thought to himself.

Being careful not to disturb the crime scene, Officer Bandeau could see that the male victim was shot multiple times and bled so profusely that he must have died very quickly. The female had been shot once in the head, killing her instantly.

There was a garage phone nearby on the wall, and he rushed over to it. He quickly called the shooting in to police headquarters. "Jake, it's Richard, number 163. There's been a fatal shooting at Marty's Garage."

His mind was going a million miles an hour as he rapidly gave the dispatch operator his shield number and his location for backup.

"I need a patrol unit and an investigator at Marty's Garage, 140 W. 51st Street. There are two bodies here: One male, one female. Recent gunshot, I heard the shots and responded. I am guarding the area now. Officers should respond to the lowest level of the garage."

"10-4, sixty three. One fifty five is in route and Investigator Sperl will respond shortly.

Headquarters then called patrol units fifty-six & sixty-seven to dispatch another patrol unit.

"Fifty-six" Officer Sanchez responds to headquarters. "Fifty six, you and sixty-seven report to West 51st Street to assist one sixty-three in his search," says dispatch. "Fifty-five will remain at the scene." Dispatcher one-ninety-three receives instructions from the Chief of Police, Walter Hadley: "Have four double units secure a ten block square perimeter around the scene immediately."

"Headquarters, one-fifty-eight, fifty-nine, sixty-one and sixty-six. Take your partners and secure a ten-block perimeter around the area in all directions, per the Chief." The four patrol units turned to respond to the crime scene. As Officer Bandeau waited for backup, he wished he had yellow crime scene tape to close off the area all around the bodies.

Without the supplies from a patrol car, he would have to wait for backup to arrive. He is very careful not to contaminate the scene as he looks around, and he notices the tire marks left from a vehicle leaving in a big hurry. The tire marks originated from a parking space, passed near the bodies and exited the parking garage. They even tracked through some of the blood as they exited the garage; a clear indication of just how fresh they were. *Somebody left here in a panic, Richard thinks.*

He also finds a small notepad near those tire tracks and inside the marked parking stall, as well as eight bullet casings near the bodies. *These two appear to be fine people, just out for the evening. They are dressed quite well; she is still holding her purse, so it is not a robbery. They were shot fairly close up and were shot intentionally*, are his thoughts. *But why? It does not make sense – they do not seem to fit any profile.*

Officer one fifty-five is Louis Lando. He arrives and confers with Richard, who points out the bullet casings, notepad, and tracks for Louis to mark with numbered tents. Louis will stay at the crime scene to tape off a fifty-foot perimeter and to perform traffic control of the site, while Richard begins to canvass the surrounding area for the shooter. It has been only been a few minutes, ten at the most, since Richard heard the shots. He notes the time in his notebook along with the other notes he has been making about the scene.

Officer Bandeau begins conducting a rapid search of the neighborhood on foot, looking in all the obvious hiding places for that shooter, hoping to discover him holed up somewhere in the vicinity. Just a few minutes later, Officers Sanchez and Jonas join Richard in his search of the neighborhood.

When the perimeter has been secured, the three officers begin canvassing the vicinity carefully, closely watching for evidence or signs of illegal entry. There is no description of the shooter; they are looking for anyone suspicious or anything out of the ordinary. Meanwhile, Investigator David Sperl is examining the crime scene, walking a two by two grid, searching for any little piece of evidence that may shed light on this case.

Over the next few hours, the investigator had fingerprinted both bodies, removed and inspected the man's wallet and her purse, had photos taken along with detailed notes. He had the bodies picked up by the coroner who arrived a few hours later.

By five o'clock the next morning, the search is halted by Chief Hadley. No sign of the perpetrator has been found and it is most likely that he has escaped their grasp for now. Chief Hadley prepared a news release to be aired on all news channels later that morning.

He planned to tell the public some of the details of this murder. It was time to enlist their help. "Someone, somewhere, knows something. The shooter is out there, and we are going to find him", vows the Chief at the end of his broadcast.

CHAPTER SIX

Jonathan Seeks Refuge

It was now two fifteen in the morning and while Jonathan had calmed down outwardly, he was still a quivering mess inwardly. The terrifying event that unfolded right before his eyes just two hours ago had him completely unhinged and unable to think clearly. He had been driving around the city without really thinking about where he was going.

Three things Jonathan did know for sure: He was not going home, he was not going to the police and he was not going to work again. He decided all that the first hour he drove around, frantically trying to stay out of sight but feeling so exposed and vulnerable. *Where can I go?* He kept asking himself. *Where will I be safe? I have got to get out of town right away. They will be looking for me - I witnessed a murder! Shit – shit – shit!*

There is no way I can continue my normal life here in NY. They will find me and it will not be pretty! I cannot go back to work; I cannot go home. What am I going to do? I have got to figure this out fast before I am discovered. The police are not the answer – that is like pouring gasoline onto the fire. They will fumble around with all their paperwork, asking the same questions over and over while I am a sitting duck at the police station.

I do not have any answers for them. I do not know who was killed, or why it happened. I just have to look out for myself! Jonathan decided what to do for the night. Marianne lived just two blocks from here. I could spend the night at her place and leave in the morning after I figured some things out.

Oh Marianne, he smiles slightly as he begins to fondly remember all the nights spent at her apartment. *Those nights I "worked overtime" were some of the best times we had. She will do this for me, but I need to keep her safe, too. I will not tell her. It will be just like the other nights we were together.*

That is not a bad plan, thinks Jonathan, and he drove toward Marianne's apartment, parking three blocks away so he did not endanger her. Jonathan rummaged through the truck looking for a screwdriver so he could remove the license plates. Watching over his shoulder for anyone looking suspicious, he was unable to find a screwdriver. Instead, he took a garden hose from the sidewalk garden and wet down some dirt so he could smear some mud on the plates, making them unreadable. Who knew how many people saw him peel out of the garage with a gun-wielding madman running after him. It was bad enough the killer saw him in the first place. *Why couldn't I have been quieter?!* Sprinting the three blocks to Marianne's, Jonathan's brain was now on fire with ideas of what he should do next.

No longer in shock, his thoughts were clearing up and a plan was beginning to form in his mind. *I will leave before daybreak and head west, out of the city and as far as I can go, as fast as I can.* Viola still lives in California if I can make it that far. She will not turn me down and no one will think to look there.

He had not seen Viola since he came home from the war. It had been a long ten years since those days. Six months they lived together in Buena Vista, California. Easy, carefree living with one of the sweetest women on Earth. Now Jonathan's mind is bringing up vivid memories of that time. *I should have just stayed out there with Viola instead of coming home to the family*, he laments.

I will not call her ahead of time. I know she still lives there because that crazy broad called my wife looking for me a couple of times. What was she thinking? Now Jonathan is chuckling over Viola. Ok, here I am. Jonathan looked around very carefully. No one seemed to be watching or following him. He approached the door and rings the bell several times before sleepy Marianne answers. "Hmm, who's that?"

"Marianne, it's me, Jonathan. Let me in!" She opened the door and Jonathan quickly ducked inside the building, hoping he would be safe for a few hours. "Hey doll, thought I would swing by for a bit. That ok with you?" "Well," she answered, "I have not seen or heard from you in a few weeks. What took you so long?" and she was all over him with loving kisses. "You are always welcome here," She responded.

"Great, but first I need some sleep, can I crawl in with you, and tomorrow we will get all caught up?" Jonathan lies to her. *By sun-up I will be long gone and in another state*, he thinks as he lays down beside Marianne. It is three AM and it does not take Jonathan long to doze off, but his sleep is fitful as images of the night's events continue to play through his mind.

CHAPTER SEVEN

Angelo Runs for It

Fast Eddy did not waste any time putting one of Tommy's hoods on the trail of Angelo. He was not about to let that worm disappear into the big city. After all, Manhattan has a million places to hide, and Eddy is a lot smarter than him. He calls his favorite shooter, the son of former mobster, Andrew Caputo, now deceased.

Gary Caputo has his head on straight and is a spot-on shooter, no matter the distance. Gary spent time in the U.S. army before joining their ranks, where he quickly learned the love of the kill. His specialty in the Army was sniper training and marksmanship. Eddy knows that one day Gary is going to be a great mercenary and that they were lucky to have him.

"Gary, report to the office at once", Eddy barks over the phone, knowing that Gary will show up within moments. Eddy would take care of the Patelli's and the eye witness himself after he cleaned up Tommy's office and got some rest. There was time for that; the cops would be on this case for hours before they got any answers.

Flatfoots are nothing more than idiot civil servants that could not make it on a regular job, he thought with sheer contempt. "Yeah," Eddy snickers, "I doubt they ever get this one right. I'm gonna make sure it is so twisted and convoluted that it makes their balls ache! ...gonna make Tommy proud!"

Not even a minute later Gary enters the office with a gleam in his eyes. He just knew this was going to be good - he could hear it in Eddy's voice. "You called me in on the Patelli case, Eddy?" he guessed. "I saw Angelo leave with his tail between his legs and I heard Tommy screaming at him."

"Yeah, I want that fucker dead! You know most of his hideouts. Run him down and bring him to me. Lock him up over at the bunker, but do not hurt him any. Just chain him up good and tight. I want all the honors for myself," sneers Eddy. "I will catch up to you later and we will go track down the Patelli's."

The bunker was a lower level cellar, below the usual cellar of the building. It was sound-proofed and designed for questioning and torturing their victims. Torture devices were installed dating back to the early 1800's.

The Heretic's Fork was popularly used for lengthy periods. This six inch metal rod had a two-pronged fork on each end. The top fork was placed just under the chin in the fleshy part, and the other end was designed to dig painfully into the bone of the sternum, thus holding the head erect at all times. Speaking was excruciating because any movement of the jaw was torturous. The individual was usually chained to the wall in an upright, standing position with the fork in place for hours at a time.

A Scold's Bridle was used on those who were found to be lying, cheating, bragging members of the criminal community. This consisted of a metal cage fastened over their head, much like a birdcage, with a long chain trailing down the back as a leash.

Inside the cage was an iron muzzle that was spiky and was inserted tightly into the mouth, piercing the tongue and causing the victim to bleed continuously from the mouth. Then the guilty party was put on display and paraded through meeting halls to suffer further humiliations and possibly even stoning or beating, depending upon the severity of the offense.

Thumb Screws were used on the most minor of offenses, but they also afflicted incredible pain. This was two spiky strips of steel fastened on each end with nuts and bolts. Both thumbs were placed in between those strips and the bolts were tightened until the person was bleeding and screaming.

Many 'treatments' were started with this device, giving the individual an opportunity to impart the needed information without more barbaric devices being used. However, people were rarely smart enough to give up the info, and the most stubborn of them often died inside Tommy's bunker.

The Whip used in the bunker was a short stick with a half dozen thin, leather straps, about eighteen inches long, protruding from one end. People were generally stripped of clothes to the waist, and the thin straps were most brutal when they had been soaked in liquid prior to use.

There were other devices in place as well, but these were the most popular ones used. This was where Tommy Two Toes spent a lot of years perfecting his brutality in his youth. When he took over from Fingers Magee, he inherited this building, along with the territory that Fingers controlled.

Eddy and Gary go their separate ways, each firmly intent on accomplishing their appointed tasks but also thinking about the major mistake made by Angelo and how he was going to pay for his stupidity.

Angelo is on the run now, speeding through city streets in his beat up Chevy Impala, cursing out loud at himself.

"You asshole! You fucking asshole! How could you make a stupid mistake like that?! This was your lucky break with Two Toes and you fucked it all up!" At that moment Angelo nearly crashed into some parked cars as he turned a corner on two wheels. Gripping the steering wheel tightly, he straightened out just in time and tried to get himself under control.

Angelo was sweating bullets and wheezing badly; he was literally scared to death. "No way I am going back to cap that fucking eye witness! Tommy will have someone waiting there for me! I ain't that stupid!" He spent the past hour driving around, and up ahead was a small parking garage he knew of.

Angelo started looking around behind him. It did not seem as if anyone was following him, so when he came to that garage he pulled in quickly and parked, burying his Chevy between two dark colored vans. *I will sit here a bit to figure things out*, he thinks.

Unknown to him, Gary was already in the garage.

Gary intuitively knew where Angelo would choose to hide first, and parked there while Angelo was racing up and down the city streets. Now Gary watches as Angelo parks his Chevy, thinking how he outwitted Tommy's thugs, and not realizing just how short his time to live really was.

Gary is wondering just what Fast Eddy has planned for Angelo's demise, and begins to envision different scenarios. *Is he going to flay him with the Whip, douse him with gasoline and set him afire?* That was Gary's favorite. *Or will Eddy pull him apart limb from limb by using the Rack, a mechanized crank that is attached to one end of the body while Angelo was securely fastened to the steel frame on the other end, stretching him until he comes apart? Hmm nice. That is even better.* Gary smiles as he see it in his mind.

Well, thinks Gary. *I am going to sit tight here a while and let Angelo believe that he pulled one over on us. Won't he be surprised when I swoop in to grab him? The little cocksucker has no idea what is coming his way. He has no clue at all, heh, heh, heh.* Gary coldly chuckles as he envisions the look on Angelo's face.

CHAPTER EIGHT

The Police Begin to Search

It is March 9, 1957 now, and Jonathan had not been home for three days. That in itself is not so unusual. Susan remembers all the times her unfaithful husband would stay away from home for weeks at a time, presumably with some other woman. Oh sure, she knew about the others. She had no details, but her Jonathan always had a keen eye for beautiful women, and he could never say no to them.

This time, however, was different. Susan could sense there was deep trouble, but she did not know exactly what the trouble was. Her sixth sense had her on high alert and feeling acutely uneasy. *What could have happened to him this time to make me feel this creepy? How is this going to affect the kids and me?*

What will we do if Jonathan does not come home at all? Now Susan's mind is reeling with possibilities, one worse than the other. "What could it be? C'mon Susan. It is probably nothing. Jonathan is out with his floozy and perhaps drinking again. He will be home when he is done playing around.

He always came home eventually." She is talking to herself now, trying to calm herself down. The kids would be home from school in an hour and she has to get hold of herself. Another thought entered her mind that brightened her outlook right away: *If nothing else, Jonathan would be home to celebrate the next three special events with us. His birthday, our wedding anniversary, and Amanda's birthday, are all grouped closely together at this time of year.*

Jonathan always loved to celebrate with us, so he would return soon enough. He was just a big kid playing in life's sandbox, but he always came home eventually. Just then the doorbell rang and Susan opened the door to find two NYPD Detectives standing there. "Oh!" she cries out as she suddenly collapses.

Detective Robert Carlson catches her and props her up until she regains her footing. "Come sit down," he urges as he leads her to the nearby couch. Susan is now crying hysterically and Detective Carlson is softly speaking to her in an attempt to calm her down.

Detective Kenneth Bentworth goes to get a cold, wet cloth from the bathroom he finds just a few steps away. He returns to the couch and places it across the back of her neck.

After a few minutes of tears, Susan manages to pull herself together and addresses the two Detectives. "Something terrible has happened to Jonathan, hasn't it?" She says. "I just knew it did not seem like all the other times. Something felt different. Something felt terribly wrong."

"Ma'am," begins the senior Detective, "we are not sure of anything just yet." Det. Carlson continues, "There was a double murder at the garage where your husband works. This happened just the other night on March 6, around midnight." Susan gasps and blurts out, "That is what time Jonathan goes off duty and heads for home!"

"Yes Ma'am, so his boss told us. Have you seen your husband since March 6th?" "No, I have not seen or heard from him. That is not unusual though. Jonathan frequently stays in the city with friends, sometimes the entire week. That is why I was not too surprised when he did not come home," answers Susan.

"Yes, Ma'am, can you provide us with the name, phone number and address of said friend?" Now Susan is crying again. When she calms down, she peers up at the very attractive Det. with her soulful blue eyes and says, "My husband is fond of women, and does not always come home.

Sometimes he is gone for days, so I was not truly alarmed. But this time I was feeling very strange about his absence. I am afraid I have no idea of who he has been seeing." "Yes, Ma'am. We have found his notebook lying on the garage floor, which is what brought us to you. That, plus his boss claims he has not been into work since the murders.

Is there any light you can shed on his whereabouts? Do you have any thoughts at all?" asks Det. Carlson. "This notebook has some very interesting remarks and notations in it. Do you know what its purpose is?" Asks Det. Carlson. Now Det. Bentworth is scribbling rapidly, trying to get it all down.

"Yes, sir, she answers. Jonathan does some handyman work for people in the area. He fixes small appliances like toasters and irons. Sometimes he takes broken items and turns them into useful lamps or whatever he can envision. Anytime thoughts come to him, Jonathan writes them down before he has a chance to forget. He also keeps a log of what project he is working on and who it is for."

"We will need to keep this notebook for analysis, Ma'am". "Yes, whatever you need. Is there anything else I can do to help? What are your thoughts about his location?" Asks Susan.

"Oh, Susan suddenly gets very loud and indignant. Surely you do not think Jonathan had anything to do with the murders!? He is not that kind of man! He may be a womanizer, but he would not hurt a fly."

"Well now Ma'am, we are just gathering facts and information, tracking down any leads that pop up. It goes without saying that you need to contact us immediately if Jonathan contacts you in any way. We will need to see him as soon as possible." The two detectives left just as Susan's children arrive from school. Their eyes are as big as dinner plates when they pass the officers on the walkway.

"Mom! Mom!" They scream, as they rush into the house. "Mom, those were cops! They were here about Daddy, weren't they! Mom! What happened to Daddy!?" Now both children were in Susan's arms and crying very hard. "Shh-shh," Susan tries to calm her children down. "Nothing has happened. Those two officers just want to ask Daddy what he saw after work a few days ago. It is nothing." Susan wishes that were the truth.

Oh, Jonathan, what have you gotten yourself into this time? Susan wonders, as she sends Michelle upstairs to waken her napping youngster, Amanda. "Michelle, you prepare dinner tonight while I finish cleaning up today's work. Jennifer, you go upstairs and do your homework. And Jennifer" - she says quite sternly – "I mean it."

After the kids have dinner and the kitchen is cleaned up, they are sent up to their bedrooms. Susan is very preoccupied now with her thoughts. *Jonathan is not coming home at all I fear, and I have to make preparations. Tomorrow I will call his boss at the garage to get more information. What am I going to do? How am I going to get through this? I have no money, no job, three small children, ...and apparently, no husband.*

CHAPTER NINE

Shattered Dreams

After leaving Susan, Detectives Carlson and Bentworth drove further east on Long Island to visit the parents of Shelby Pratel, who were living in Northport. They wanted to make sure there was no more information on the Pratel's lifestyle, acquaintances, friends or close family. They did not want to miss anything that might shed some light on what happened or why.

Bill and Shirley Pratel had been contacted two days ago and actually identified the bodies. The funeral had been planned for tomorrow, and Det. Carlson wanted to gather details before any more time passed. He knew that as grief and sorrow sets in, memory often fades away for a time - at least until some of the pain has healed.

Often the grieving survivors of a shocking crime will become dysfunctional to the point of being incoherent and unable to think rationally. Det. Carlson had learned that Bill and Shirley were originally from Alabama and had moved to New York when Shelby relocated five years ago. They were a small, close knit family and purchased homes within a block of each other.

Shelby had proven to his parents that he was capable and wise in everything he attempted and, as sons go, Bill could not imagine anyone finer. Shelby even found the perfect wife to partner with. Bill was at home in the front yard when the detectives arrived. "Please come on in," Bill said in a sad voice, "we will join the missus on the back porch where she is resting." Now Bill really looked them over, saying, "This has been quite a shock for her, don't you know."

"Yes, sir, I am very sorry for the intrusion," answered Det. Bentworth. "Honey, those nice detectives are back," says Bill as they step out onto the porch. You remember Detectives Carlson and Bentworth?" "Yes," Shirley replies with a quivering lip. In a moment she is in tears again, but she pulls herself together and looks the officers squarely in the eyes and says, "I want you to find the man who killed my Shelby and that darling wife of his.

Those two were the nicest couple anywhere!" "Yes, ma'am. We are sorry to disturb you at this time but we also want to find who did this." Det. Carlson continues, "We have a thirteen state All Points Bulletin issued on a person of interest who may have witnessed the crime, and we expect to get critical details once he is located."

Detective Carson is interviewing both parents now, while Det. Bentworth takes notes. "Tell me what kind of work they did." "Well," answers Bill, "Shelby was the local minister down at the Gospel Church of East Northport. He was accepted there about five years ago and was very occupied with growing the church membership. That church only had about fifty members when my Shelby arrived, but now there is over two hundred people there!"

"I see," says Det. Carlson. "What about his other job - I understand there was not enough money to support them through the church, and he had to work someplace else." Shirley answers now, "I brought

Shelby and Candi over to Laura's Child Care Center, just down on Main St.

They both worked there part time - Candi loved taking care of the little ones and Shelby did minor maintenance work as needed. Shelby also did part time maintenance work at Telephonics when they called him in."

Shirley begins to cry again, "They both loved children so much! They were planning a family, and she was already trying to get pregnant!" "What were they doing in the city that night? Who were they meeting?" Det. Carlson now directs these questions back to Bill.

"There was no meeting in New York. The only people they knew in New York were the organizers for that big soup kitchen down in Harlem. Shelby and Candi spent several evenings each month as volunteers, especially in the cold winter season. They went to the city for Candi's birthday - she just turned thirty two. He loved to take her to dinner and then the theater. They usually ate at Sardi's when they went to the city - it was a special treat for them.

My son had plans, you know. Shelby had big dreams for that church of his. He saw that church becoming a true spiritual anchor on Long Island. Candi had a music background and the sweetest singing voice you ever heard. She was going to be the music director. They wanted to bring children in from the inner city neighborhoods for Sunday school so the kids could experience something joyous and wonderful at least once in a while.

Church growth only happens when there are families involved, my son was fond of saying. They worked so damn hard! Why! Oh, God, Why!" Bill exclaimed as he also broke into tears. "Why did you take my boy away!?"

Both detectives saw there was nothing more to be learned so they left quietly, pausing just to place a consoling hand on Bill's Shoulder. As they went out to their car, they could hear Shirley crying.

CHAPTER TEN

On the Run

After a short and fitful sleep, Jonathan gets up quietly; Marianne does not stir at all as he heads to the bathroom. He washes up quickly, and thinks, *Hmm, I should shave my hair off to change my appearance. And I will leave my beard so I look scruffy. That might help,"* he thinks, as he stares into the mirror. *Where did I leave that razor... yep, here it is. This will not take long."*

Fifteen minutes later, dressed and ready to go, Jonathan takes one more longing look at Marianne, wishing he could stay. *Goodbye sweetheart,* he thinks, as he quietly goes out the door. It is five thirty AM and still dark out as he gets into his pickup truck. He drives off in the direction of Pennsylvania, still busy with thoughts of how to get out of this mess. A four-part plan is beginning to take shape in his mind, and it does not include going home, ever again.

Ok, time to implement part one of this plan; get out of town! Jonathan turns on an all-news radio station, WCBS, to see if he hears anything about last night. After two hours of listening, the station loses its reception and he turns it off. He did not hear a word about the murders on the news, but *that does not mean that no one is looking for me.*

AT A MOMENT'S NOTICE

The cops may not be looking for me yet, but they will as soon as they talk to my boss. And certainly, the killer is looking for me! I wonder if anyone has contacted Susan yet. Gee, I will miss the kids. Michelle, Amanda and Jennifer are going to be beauties; the boys will be lining up to date them. I hope Susan raises them to be smart and choosy when it comes to boys!

The kids were great fun; I always enjoyed being around them - especially Jennifer. What a little tomboy she is! She is scrappy; Jennifer gets into trouble no matter what she is trying to do. And, she is a good looking charmer. Guess she is gonna be just like me; too bad I will not be around to see her grow up. I would have liked that, he sighs. Well, it cannot be helped - I gotta get lost. Sorry kids...

When I got dressed this morning I did not find my little notebook that I always carry. I hope I did not drop it last night, because that will lead the cops, and the killer, right to Susan. I want Susan to be safe - as a wife, she was a pain in the ass; always pushing me to do stuff - but I do not wish her any harm. Well, I cannot do anything about that now.

Ok, here is a busy truck stop where I can get some breakfast, and a lot of coffee to go. Half an hour later, Jonathan is on the road again. Some hours later, as he sees the tall trees and countryside pass, Jonathan sees that he is deep into Pennsylvania now - almost to Ohio. *Wow! What time is it? Uh, almost three PM. I have been on the road for almost ten hours. No wonder my back hurts.*

I need to stretch. Guess I have been lost in thought, I am so tired; I should be paying closer attention to who is behind me, Jon thinks, and immediately checks to see if someone is following him. *There does not seem to be anyone after me yet.* Soon as I get to Chicago, I am implementing part two of my plan. I cannot leave any kind of trail, no one must be able to find me. This will work but I have to be tricky and alert. I cannot just make a straight run to California. I need to be smarter than them.

"When I get to Chicago I will get some sleep," he says to himself. "I will be in Chicago soon... Push on for now, halfway there." Some time later, Jon is getting very drowsy. All of a sudden he hears a long, loud honk, "Oh shit!" he exclaims. Then he realized he had been drifting into the other lane.

I have to stay alert, I must keep my mind active, or I will kill myself before I get to Chicago. I will think about Viola. "Oh, darling, I will be home again soon. We will have some grand times, you and I. Bet you are still as pretty as ever! If there is a time when I have to run again, I am taking you with me," Jon says to himself.

"You are definitely the one to keep! You never annoyed me, and together we had plenty of fun. You could always make me laugh... We will run off so far, they will never find me... I must rest and think things through. Hmm," Jonathan frowns. "I wonder who that killer was and why he murdered that nice looking couple. I wonder - nah - couldn't be a mob hit.

What would the Mafia have to do with someone like that? Who were they? Hmm, better see if I can get another news station on the radio. I should be close enough to town for the radio to work." "Good evening, folks, this is Ben Stiles at WJKR Fort Wayne, Indiana, and we are talking about the recent murders in New York City of a local minister and his wife.

A moment ago, our caller, Dave, said how glad he is that he does not live in, and I quote, 'The Great City of Death'. I have Dave on the line with me, and he has agreed to tell us why he calls NYC by that name. Dave, are you there?" "Yes, Ben, I am here," answers Dave. "Please tell us why you have nicknamed NYC the 'Great City of Death.'

"Well, every day another violent crime in New York is announced on the news. Crime must be rampant there. I would not live there for fear of my life. According to today's newspaper, the murdered couple were just visiting for the evening. You know, taking in the sights, like normal people do. He was pastor of a church, for Pete's sake! ..."

Jonathan turned the radio off. He had heard enough – it is all over the news. *No word of him yet, but that will come out eventually. I really do need to sleep. The next lonely patch of woods I find on this route, I will park deep inside and take a little rest. After all, it has been fourteen hours now. Then I will finish my drive. A pastor, huh? Who would want to kill a pastor...?*

Thirty minutes later, there is a wooded area. *I am pulling in.* Five minutes later Jonathan was deep in the woods where no one could find him. He closed his eyes and within moments he was fast asleep. He never noticed the vehicle that pulled in after him...

CHAPTER ELEVEN

Officer Bandeau is Full of Surprises

When Officer Richard Bandeau first discovered the Pratels' bodies on that fateful night, his most heartfelt desire was to be an integral part of the investigation. He had wanted to become an investigator since he was a young cadet, and he was going to make it happen on this case, even if Chief Hadley did not assign him to the case.

It was readily apparent the next day that Richard was not to be a part of the investigating team, so he immediately took a leave of absence. His plan was to work the case on his own and on the sly. He just knew that the witness was a key piece to the puzzle, and Richard planned to track him down to get the answers.

The morning after the murders, Richard returned in his street clothes to the parking garage to speak to the owner, Marty Grains. Marty spoke freely when questioned by Richard, giving a complete description of both Jonathan and the vehicle he drives. "Jonathan is about six feet tall with wavy brown hair, slender and very good looking.

He has no visible scars or tattoos. His pickup truck is tan colored, a Ford, I believe. I have the license plate in Jonathan's employee records. "Hmm . . . let me see, yes, here it is: A Ford truck from NY, it is H129." Marty and Jonathan had many chuckles in the past over the women in their lives, so he also knew where Jonathan often spent his nights in the city.

Marty gives the approximate street address for Marianne's residence to the officer. Both men were assuming that Jonathan would not be going home, and Richard knew that he did not go to the police. Marianne's would be the logical starting point in tracking down Jonathan. Richard was able to locate Marianne's apartment after questioning some of her neighbors.

In fact, Jonathan's pickup truck was seen last night, three blocks away, and Jonathan was watched as he covered the plates with mud. That act seemed very suspicious to the young man who witnessed it, so he followed Jonathan to see where he was going.

The curious neighbor simply attributed it to an illicit affair after seeing Jonathan's behavior and the way he entered the apartment, swiveling his head around as if expecting to see someone else. Funny, he did not spot the neighbor in the bushes across the way.

Upon questioning Marianne it was obvious to Officer Bandeau that she knew nothing at all of the murders or of Jonathan's involvement, if any. Her reaction was one of complete surprise and concern for Jonathan's welfare. Being a witness to such a terrible crime could only lead to dire consequences once the killer located such a witness.

Because of her fear for Jonathan's safety, Marianne was more than happy to give a complete accounting of his brief visit and his description as well. She does not know that Jonathan shaved his head, changing his appearance somewhat, but she hands Richard one of the photos she has of Jonathan. Then she took it one step further: "I bet he is going to hide out until that whole situation is resolved. Jonathan's not real fond of confrontation. When facing anything uncomfortable, he turns the other way.

"Ya know, he used to talk about a gal in California; a girlfriend he lived with after the war. Now what was her name...?" Marianne begins pacing around her small apartment, trying to remember what Jonathan called the woman he lived with ten years ago. "I cannot think of it right now, but it will come to me. Vivian? Violet? Umm, it begins with a 'V'."

I do not know the last name. I would not be a bit surprised if he shows up out there." Several moments go by, then she blurts out, "Oh, I know! Her name is Viola!" Richard hands Marianne his card and asks her to please call him as further details come to her mind, and he thanks her for assisting him in his investigation.

Officer Bandeau's next step is to plot out an initial course to California from NYC, making a basic, educated guess as to Jonathan's chosen route. He is going to see if he can catch up to Jonathan. Marianne is surely right in thinking that Jonathan will run to familiar territory as far from New York as he can get. He drives across the George Washington Bridge, crosses into Pennsylvania, and is rapidly formulating an action plan in his mind.

Driving very fast, he thinks that Jonathan might not be driving so fast himself - he would not want to draw attention to himself by speeding. Richard also figures that Jonathan will not be making too many stops along the way, but he will need food and coffee if Marianne's account of just a nap is true.

The guy has probably been awake for two days straight, except for that nap at Marianne's. He will be putting distance between himself and the killer, and the cops as well. Richard decides to stop at the first busy truck stop he comes to so he can ask questions. Jonathan will want a busy place so he can avoid being remembered.

After another hour, Richard pulls into a very large truck stop with lots of traffic. Upon entering, he immediately seeks the manager to ask permission to question the waitresses. Receiving that permission, Richard searches for the girls who worked the previous day. Giving Jonathan's description, one waitress immediately indicates that she served him.

"It was shortly after our breakfast rush, and he ordered sandwiches and coffee to go. He went to the men's room and then left right after paying the bill. But your picture is not exactly accurate.

I mean, it sure looks like him, except he was bald and had a scraggly beard." Richard updates his notes on Jonathan's description and thanks the waitress, leaving her his card with directions to please call him with further information if she thinks of anything else.

He then leaves the truck stop, driving as fast as he dares on the Pennsylvania highway. Officer Bandeau feels elated certainty that he is heading in the right direction and wants to catch up before Jonathan disappears too deeply into the countryside.

Several hours later, Richard cannot believe his eyes when he believes he spots Jonathan's pickup truck down the road a bit. *Could it be? Is it possible that he actually guessed correctly, and this is the man that everyone is looking for?*

He slows down a bit so he does not startle Jonathan as he comes up a little closer for a good look. Yes, it is a tan Ford, and the license plate is NY H129 - *Oh my God, I did it! I caught up to him! What an incredible stroke of luck! Ok, now back off. I do not want to scare him off so I will just tag along way back here. Son of a gun!*

Jonathan was driving a bit erratically, indicating severe exhaustion. Richard could see that he was having a hard time staying in place on the road, and his speed was not consistent, either. "He must be really tired by now. His attention span will not be good either, so he probably will not notice me if I stay a good distance away from him."

In just two more hours, Jonathan slows way down and pulls off into the wooded area beyond the edge of the road. *Yes*, thinks Richard, *he is going to hide so he can sleep for a while. And I am going to crawl in there after him.*

CHAPTER TWELVE

Angelo's Capture

Gary was chuckling to himself while he waited for Angelo to calm down and doze off in his car. Relaxed and thinking he had not been followed to the garage, Angelo closed his eyes and fell asleep. And the truth was, he was not followed, but rather, Gary knew the predictable move Angelo would make and was waiting at the garage, watching for Angelo to arrive.

It had only been an hour, and sure enough - Angelo began nodding off. *You cannot hide from me*, Gary silently sneered. Now that the time was perfect, Gary put his plan in action. He quietly moved his car into place, blocking Angelo's vehicle. There would be no escape for Angelo.

Carefully closing his car door, Gary approached from the passenger side of Angelo's car and peered in. Just as he thought, Angelo was asleep. Gary threw open the door, reached in and dragged the sleepy Angelo out onto the garage floor before Angelo knew what was happening.

Gary stuffed a small towel in Angelo's mouth as he opened it to scream, and although he fought back, it was futile against Gary's brute strength. Gary proceeded to hogtie him with duct tape, both hands and feet behind him. It was a bit of a struggle to secure Angelo by himself, so Gary gave him a solid punch in the gut, which left Angelo gasping for air. He stopped squirming and quieted down.

Angelo began to moan as he lay on the cold garage floor. Gary kicked him hard, right in the kidneys, and hollered at him, "Shut the fuck up, asshole!" Gary threw Angelo into the trunk of his Chrysler and drove to Tommy's secret torture bunker. Mindful that Tommy claimed exclusive rights to punish Angelo, Gary was careful not to rough him up too much.

He did not want any marks to show on Angelo, incurring Tommy's wrath. Upon arrival at Tommy's shop, Gary grabbed the mechanics dolly, a flat, four wheeled dolly used by mechanics to roll under a car, and threw Angelo on top of it, tying him down securely so he could roll the squirrely bastard over to the elevator, and then to the secret bunker.

Gary was glad that Tommy had given him the chance to do this important job so he could show off his capable skills. Once inside the bunker, Gary released the hogtie and chained Angelo securely to the brick wall, cinching the chains very tightly so Angelo would have no room to move about and was forced to remain standing. *That is gonna hurt*, thought Gary as he walked away.

With that accomplished, Gary reported back to Fast Eddy, who in turn let Tommy know that he had a special visitor in the bunker. Tommy was in no hurry, preferring to let Angelo hang in there for a while, letting him wonder about his fate. Angelo certainly was worried about what he was in for.

Surely, it would not be good. Most likely, he would not survive. He was determined to stay strong, but already, his limbs were shaking from the strain and deep fear. "Oh God," he moaned, "I hope I do not wet myself. Dear God, help me out here, please. I know I am not an upstanding guy, but please let it be quick," Angelo prayed.

He knew this was the worst possible trouble he could be in. "Why, oh why did I take Tommy's job offer?" He lamented. In Tommy's office there was a lot of joking going on amongst the three gangsters, Tommy, Eddy and Gary. "Woo-hoo!" Hollered Tommy Two Toes. "We are gonna have us some fun tonight! Can you imagine that little punk trying to pull one over on me? Just wait 'til I get in there, nose to nose with that idiot.

First, he will learn his lesson. And he will learn it well. Then, he will *not* live to regret it. Heh, heh, heh. Eddy, go find the Patelli's home and take care of that deed. I do not want to hear anything except, 'It is done.' Got it?" "Ok, Boss", replies Eddy as he checks his gun, grabs his jacket and quickly leaves the office.

"Gary, you are gonna go fishing at the police precinct. Be smart about it; find out what they know about that witness and where the fuck he got to. Maybe they have him under wraps already. If they do, find out where he is holed up. Get to that location and bring him to me. I do not care how you do it - I need to know what he told the cops and who he told it to. Then we can tie up any loose ends."

"Right away," answers Gary as he takes off, planning his next step. After Tommy dismisses his two best men, he goes back to his office to wrap up his paperwork for the day. He plans to go home for a bit before handling the Angelo issue. Lucinda, his sexy wife, has been complaining lately that he is not home enough, and Tommy wants to keep her happy.

He really is crazy about that broad. He does not understand it, but she has a certain way about her that drives him nuts and keeps him interested. After another thirty minutes, Tommy leaves his office with a smile on his face; he is thinking about Lucinda again.

She is a lively one, both in the sack and also when dealing with life's issues. It is the first relationship he has ever had where he wanted to be faithful - imagine that! *I will come back here after midnight to visit with Angelo, I cannot wait to hear his blood curling screams and pitiful begging*, thinks Tommy.

CHAPTER THIRTEEN

Taking Stock

Susan knows in her heart that Jonathan's not coming home. It is just a strong feeling she has, that he will use this as an excuse to leave his family and move on. Susan was confiding in Berta, her good friend and occasionally her children's babysitter. Berta was from Sweden, and very old fashioned. She lived a short distance from Susan and the two women enjoyed their infrequent visits.

"I know Jonathan all too well - he has never been Mr. Dependable - although he does love the kids. If he comes home I will be very surprised. How could he do that to them? Damn him anyway - is this just an excuse for him to move on? I should never have trusted him. Should never have married him! I want to know what happened."

Berta asks, "Why can he not just report what he saw to the police and be done with it? Why does the family have to suffer like this? The kids will be devastated if he does not come home. What are you going to do? You are not prepared to be a single working mother with three small children."

"I'm trying to figure it out", Susan tells Berta. "Is he dead? Did the Mafia find him and finish him off? Will I ever know for sure? When the police finally figure it all out, will they even tell me the truth? Oh my God, these kinds of questions are going to drive me mad!"

Now Susan is thinking out loud. I need to stick to the current issues. I have got to prepare now. I will make a list of things to get done.

There is nothing like a good list to organize the current problems, making them more manageable and less intimidating. That is how I get things done on this home construction project, too.

Susan says to Berta, "It is all too scary. I only have fifteen dollars in my pocket and no savings account to tap into. We will need groceries in a few days and Jon has the only car that is running.

There are six cars in the back yard right now that need a little work to get them running again. I can get some cash for those cars, and I would have some ready cash for grocery money. I'll keep one for my own transportation."

Susan turns to Berta and asks, "Do you know who I could talk to about selling these cars?" "Yes, Berta responds. There's a junk man named Cowboy Al who takes all kinds of things for a negotiated price. You might not get much, but I suppose it's better than nothing. Susan", Berta continues, "don't you have extra property?"

"You might be able to sell off some of your land. Would you consider that? Plus, I saw a help wanted sign in the window of the local diner. Maybe they'll hire you as a waitress."

"Thanks, Berta" Susan responds. "I'll apply today, and I'll think about the property. That's exactly the kind of help I need."

"I'll need a babysitter while I'm working. You'll help out with that, won't you Berta?"

"Of course! I'm always glad to watch your kids. If there's anything else, you just let me know." With that said, the two friends ended their conversation.

Now Susan is remembering the promising career she left behind in the city. *Until Jonathan asked me to marry him, I was on track for becoming a premiere opera singer at the Metropolitan Opera House in New York City.* Crying now, she thinks *I had passed my tryouts and everything. My life could have been so much sweeter, more exciting and rewarding at the opera.*

I could have traveled far and wide as a singer with the Troupe. Susan sighs in a dreamy way - *champagne and roses every night. There were so many suitors lining up and I just told them, no thanks, I am engaged to be married. That is what I gave up for you, Jonathan. How could I have been so stupid!*

Angry now, Susan has no happy thoughts for her husband. *You bastard! You damn well better come home! How dare you leave me here with this mess! Humph! If the Mafia does not kill you - I just might do it myself!*

CHAPTER FOURTEEN

Timing is Everything

Fast Eddy had been dispatched to Northport, Long Island, to take care of the Patelli's, and what he found upon his arrival was a mystery. The home was abandoned by the family who lived there, including their pets. He found evidence of dogs living there, probably two, judging by the food dishes and doggie beds. *These rich Long Islanders actually have very fancy stuff for their damn dogs*, thinks Eddy.

He went from room to room, looking at everything, marveling at the sheer number of books in the house. *Who reads that much?* He wonders, as he rifles through the pages of each book, looking for any pertinent information. *My own reading material consists of Penthouse and Playboy*, he thinks with a wide grin. Eddy also goes through the garbage in each room, making sure he does not miss anything.

In the living room, Eddy is carefully going through the desk in the corner. Gee, all these bills stacked up here, and they are all paid in full. *This guy makes a rather large wage*, thinks Eddy. *I hate guys like this. Rich, so they think they do not have to follow the rules. They look down on us common folks and will not even acknowledge our existence.* Still looking *through the desk, he finds a small notebook. What's this? An address book! This can be very promising. Tommy will be very pleased with this find.*

To Eddy, it appeared that everyone, including the children, have their own bedroom. *These are rich cats indeed! Let us see now, Mom and Dad have the large bedroom with their own bathroom. Look here, they have matching bathrobes. Well, isn't that sweet,* Eddy growls. *Ok, this bedroom belongs to a little girl, it says Wanda on the door. Lots of books in here, too. Oh, look - she has a cat named Blackie; there's a picture on her dresser.*

That cat sleeps with her; the cat's black fur is all over the white bedspread. Nice, he sneers. *What do you need with a cat when you already have a pussy,* Eddy says under his breath with a sinister tone. *Just wait 'til I get my hands on you - I have not had any hot, sweet, virgin pussy in ages! I hope you are not any older than ten!* Everyone knew that Eddy is one of the most depraved guys on Tommy's team.

Oh, there is another bathroom here! Well, guess you can't have enough of them, Eddy thinks with a smirk. *Rich folks... At my house, there are a dozen people sleeping wherever they find a spot, and there is only one bathroom. We do ok; everybody is happy. And this bedroom must be for a young boy.* After carefully going through that room, Eddy says, "Tommy, Tommy, you are not doing your schoolwork.

Just look at these poor grades. Forty seven percent for math - even I did better than that! Pretty soon you will be old enough to join our organization and I will teach you how to become just like our very own Tommy Two Toes. Aah, fresh meat to train!" After a thorough search of the house, basement, garage and yard, Eddy is indeed, puzzled.

Where could they be? It looks like they left in the middle of a meal, which is sitting cold on the dining room table. They did not take any clothes with them; the closets are full and Eddy found luggage for each of them, labeled and neatly stacked in the basement. *What the fuck? Where are they?*

Now Eddy is sitting on the back porch, rocking back and forth on the patio chair, considering all that he has found out here. *Clearly they know something is up. Someone told them to get out of town; to go hide away. The place is so clean! There are no messages laying around, no hints of any kind. Just that address book - their first mistake.*

After what seemed like a long time, Eddy goes back inside to look at the newspaper he saw in the living room. *Yep, it is today's paper with news of the Pratels' murder. These are smart people, really smart. They must have figured it out. That hit was really meant for Patelli, not Pratel. And that means that Patelli is definitely on the run, hiding his family for protection. Damn, they even took the stupid pets!*

Running with the pets - well, that will make it easier to find them if they plan to use any kind of hotel or motel. Not many of those establishments take pets, Eddy thought smugly. *Your second mistake, asshole.* "I am gonna track you down and have my way with your daughter. And you are gonna watch every minute of it.

If she pleases me I may let her live so I can enjoy her again and again. Then I am gonna do the Momma, and you will watch that, too," Eddy says with glee. "I will take care of your stupid ass in front of the whole family. The boy is worthy of a looky-loo by Tommy - maybe we can use him.

Oh man, sweet payday is almost here!" Eddy is howling with sinister laughter as he gets back into his car to begin his search for the Patelli's using the address book that he discovered in the living room desk.

CHAPTER FIFTEEN

Plan B

When Samuel Patelli read about the Pratel's murder in the late edition newspaper the day after it happened, he was instantly on the alert. While he did not know the Pratels personally, he was aware of who they were in the small, close-knit community; he had seen them at church.

Their murder did not make any sense at all, and Sam was pretty sure that a mistake had been made by the killer. This set Sam on edge because he sensed that the hit was meant for his family. It had to be his testimony. The paper was not very clear about who the murderer was, but since Sam and his wife, Carolyn, had recently testified in court against the mobster Tommy Carudente, Sam was making the assumption that they were in grave danger.

There were just too many parallel facts between the two families. He knew as soon as Tommy realized the error, he would come after the Patelli's. Sam decided to call David Sperl, the lead investigator on the Tommy Carrudente case, immediately. He left an urgent message for the detective's attention: Call Sam Patelli immediately regarding the Pratel murders.

Sam does not want to alarm his family, but he does realize the danger they are in and tells his wife what is going on, and to prepare the family to leave. "Do not pack anything, we will make better time without luggage. Close up the house and be sure to pack Tommy's medicine.

We will take the dogs and cat to the boarding kennel and prepay for two weeks; I do not want to travel with them. I do not know when we will return, so call the school and tell them we are on vacation. You take care of those details while I speak to Det. Sperl, and we will leave as soon as the kids are home from school. We have one hour, go!"

"What about dinner?" Asks Carolyn. The food is already cooked; should we eat first?" No sooner than those words were spoken, Det. Sperl called Sam. While Sam answers the phone, Carolyn puts dinner on the table. "Sam, I was just about to call you anyway," says Det. Sperl. "Have you seen the news? There has been a mob hit and I want to place you and your family under protective custody for a while.

I have a place arranged for you and I am sending a car to pick you up. I have a unit of two men assigned to your family from a select group of mine. You should plan on staying until this is over and the killer is in custody." "Thank God," Sam says as he breathes a sigh of relief. "Those poor people were gunned down! I know it was meant for us, I feel it in my bones. We will be ready within the hour, as soon as the kids are home from school."

Det. Sperl responds, "No delays, and do not bring anything that is not necessary. We need to get you under cover, pronto. My officers are on the way. Do not open the door for anyone except for Sargents Whitfield and Belafonte. Insist on seeing their badges. Is that clear?" "Yes, sir," Sam responds with a shaky voice. "Thank you!"

Sam rushes over to Carolyn, who is putting the kitchen in order. He grabs her from behind and gives her a tight squeeze. His tears are flowing now as pent up nervousness is released. "Honey, I love you and the kids so much," Sam chokes out. "I just need you to know that I am so sorry for putting us all in a perilous situation, but I wanted to do the right thing. Please, let us pray that we get through this all right."

And with that, the children arrived home from school, instantly clamoring for Mom's and Dad's attention, everyone speaking at once. Carolyn instructs them to change their clothes because they are going on a little vacation, which raises all kinds of questions from Tommy and Wanda.

"Never mind," she says to them. "It is a surprise, just go get ready because we are leaving in a few minutes. Put your favorite game in your bag." Thank goodness she had packed an emergency bag of essentials for the family. As the kids went to their room, she calls out, "Put on your sneakers!"

While Carolyn and the kids got ready, Sam puts their pets in his car and takes them to the kennel. Since arrangements were made earlier over the phone by Carolyn, this was a simple drop off. Sam was nervous and frightened driving the short distance. The last thing he needed was to be caught out here by the killer.

Sam did not know if the house was being watched and thought it would be safer to take the pets to the kennel without his family. After an uneventful drop off, Sam makes it home, just ahead of the police. "Ok," he says to himself with a heavy sigh of relief, "we are on our way to safety." He thanks God in his heart and goes inside the house to gather his family and take them to safety.

CHAPTER SIXTEEN

Tommy's Wrath

Several hours ago, Tommy sent his two hoods, Eddy and Gary, on errands, and he has not heard from Eddy yet. He was sent to dispose of the Patelli family, and Gary was to locate that eye witness. Gary is standing in front of him now. His search for that eye witness proved fruitless.

Gary did go to the police precinct to visit with Officer Sanchez, a cop who had been on the take for as long as he was on the force. Sanchez and Gary went way back and the two men often traded facts for favors. Now Sanchez reported to Gary that the eye witness was a ghost. He never showed up at any medical facilities in the area, nor did he arrive to make any report to the police.

So far the thirteen state APB had rendered no information at all, and no sightings of this guy. If he had not been married and working, one would almost say he did not exist. Maybe they should speak to the wife, thinks Gary. Gary did not like that he had to disappoint Tommy, but it was time to report in.

So here he stood, just after midnight, and Tommy did not like what he was hearing. He started to growl his response but stopped short.

"What does it really matter? We know where the Patelli's are and Eddy is disposing of them at this very moment. That witness only knows about Angelo, and he has no knowledge of our involvement." Tommy stares hard at Gary and harshly says, "C'mon, let's go take care of this bastard, Angelo. I been looking forward to this all fucking night."

The two men go down into the bowels of the building where Tommy's bunker is housed. They find Angelo still tightly chained to the wall in an upright position, and very close to unconscious. As soon as Angelo hears Tommy approaching, he snaps out of it and stiffens up. Angelo knows he is about to die a horrible death, but he decided hours ago that he would not even whimper. He was going to go out as a man, no matter what they did to him.

"Hey asshole!" Tommy screams at Angelo, who refuses to recognize that with an answer. "Hey! I'm talking to you!" Tommy gives Angelo a sharp kick in the groin this time, which elicits a loud "Whuh!" from Angelo. He is still chained to the wall and cannot fall over, but now he is slumped forward a bit and breathing with great difficulty.

Tommy gives Gary direction to release Angelo's chains and haul him over to the Rack, attaching him tightly to the device that is going to tear him limb from limb. While Angelo is tightly gritting his teeth in an effort to stay quiet, he is wondering how he will get through this pain without giving Tommy any satisfying screams.

"You are gonna pay for your incompetence, you stupid, fucking moron!" Screams Tommy. "If you could not do the job, you should never have come to me! I hate incompetent idiots!" Now Tommy is coming over to where Angelo is secured to the Rack and he is wielding a very sharp pair of wire cutters, with which he is threatening Angelo's right ring finger.

Angelo's eyes grow very big with fear, but still there is no sound from him. This fact further infuriates Tommy who snaps off that finger in anger. Then another finger, and still another one. Angelo grunts in pain through his clenched teeth with a loud "Nyuh!", but still, no whining and no tears. Angelo remains strong, his mind focused on his wife and children instead of the excruciating pain.

Tommy orders Gary to grab the whip hanging on the wall nearby and start flaying Angelo's legs and upper torso. The sound of that whip could clearly be heard in the large cavernous room as Gary applies it with force, but there is very little response from the white-faced, trembling Angelo.

A few tears have escaped and run down his face, but he is still not showing much reaction, other than the deep grimace on his face. On the inside, however, Angelo is gripped with terrifying fear and unbelievably intense agony. Angelo is now thoroughly soaked in blood, but is still not giving Tommy the sick pleasure of hearing him scream.

Tommy is now berserk with anger. He is screaming at Angelo, "You are gonna pay, dammit! I want to hear you beg for your life, you stupid motherfucker!" But Angelo's eyes are shut tightly and at this point he is barely able to stay conscious. He is praying to pass out soon. Gary receives orders from the outraged Tommy to begin turning the rack, and while he begins cranking, Tommy takes his cutters to Angelo's vulnerable manhood, castrating him and stuffing it in his mouth.

At that point, Angelo finally opens his eyes wide and tries to scream but his mouth is filled with his own member. Although it seems like an eternity, it is just another moment before he dies. At the death of Angelo, Gary sees Tommy's face turn beet red with rage. Tommy is screaming incomprehensibly, throwing anything within his reach at the walls.

His eyes light up with a most wicked gleam when he spots the old machete hanging on the wall. Grabbing that tool, Tommy slashes away at Angelo's dead body again and again while Gary steps far away in fear of being slashed himself. About five minutes later, Tommy stops.

He is soaked with sweat and completely drained of emotion. Turning to Gary he says, "Take out this garbage, turn out the lights and lock up. I will see you in my office tomorrow; make it after lunch." Then Tommy goes home to clean up and nurse his wounded ego, muttering under his breath.

When Gary got busy with Angelo's unrecognizable remains, he said respectfully, "You paid Tommy back, Angelo. The fact that Tommy's torture did not reduce you to a worthless, stinking pile of dog shit is going to bother him for a long time. Good for you, Angelo. You took it like a man."

CHAPTER SEVENTEEN

In the Woods

Officer Richard Bandeau has pulled into the woods and is not far behind Jonathan's pickup truck. There is just enough space to remain secretive and hidden from Jonathan's view. Richard is sure that Jon wants to catch a nap before continuing on to his destination, but that is not going to happen.

Richard is feeling a strong surge of adrenaline as he quietly gets out of his vehicle and makes his way through the woods to Jonathan's truck. His gun is drawn as he approaches the driver's side of the truck, peering in to see that Jonathan is fast asleep, snoring up a storm. Any louder and they would hear him on the moon.

Let's see, thinks Richard. I will wake him up, handcuff him and place him in my backseat. Then I will call headquarters from the nearest police precinct to let them know that I have located their key witness. Yes, he thinks. I will take him to Fort Wayne, the nearest city. They can hold him for proper transport back to New York City.

Wow! I have really found him! Ok, down to business – I am not there yet. Let's not make a mistake by getting ahead of myself. No one knows I am out here, and this guy could possibly be dangerous. Richard approaches the truck with his gun drawn and yells at Jonathan in his deep authoritative police voice, "This is the police!" Jonathan jumps up, startled.

"Put your hands on the steering wheel!" Slowly, Jonathan sits up, puts his hands on the wheel and says, "What? Who's there? Who are you? What do you want?" In a shaky voice. Richard yells, "Police! Let me see your driver's license! Careful now; no quick moves," he cautions.

"Yes sir", he says as he slowly withdraws his license from his wallet and hands it over. Seeing that this is truly Jonathan Anthony, Richard orders him out. "Step out of the car with your hands up!" Jonathan is now wide awake, eyes darting around frantically. Seeing no possible escape, he answers, "Ok. Ok officer, I'm coming out!"

Jonathan exits the vehicle with his hands held out in front of him, clearly showing that they are empty. "What is going on, officer?" He asks very innocently. Richard conducts a thorough search on Jonathan, patting him down, looking for weapons, then orders: "Get down on the ground!"

As Jonathan complies, Richard tells him who he is. "I am Officer Bandeau with the New York City Police Department. You are being taken into custody for questioning with regard to the murders of Shelby and Candice Pratel on the evening of March 6, 1957. Do you understand what I'm talking about?"

"Yes sir," Jonathan responds as Richard handcuffs him and hauls him to his feet. "But it was not me! I did not do it!" "You can tell me all about it at police headquarters!" Richard says to him. At that point, Jonathan falls silent and begins to think, *What now? How the heck did this guy find me?*

"Just get in the car; like I said, we will talk at headquarters," says Richard, as he securely fastens Jonathan to the door in the back seat, opposite the driver's seat. Next, he begins to drive back to Fort Wayne, Indiana. His mind is racing with elation. *He found Jonathan Anthony!*

CHAPTER EIGHTEEN

A New Resolve

It has been another week without Jonathan, but I am managing quite well, Susan thought, a little happy with herself. Jonathan had run off in the Ford pickup truck, leaving several old vehicles in the yard in various forms of disrepair. The easiest one to fix was the Willey's Jeep, which had only been out of commission for a week or two.

All it needed was new tires and a wheel alignment, and it was ready to go. That was Susan's first choice and had it repaired since it was an inexpensive fix and put her in a vehicle right away. She was not fond of driving the darn thing - it was like handling a tank! But the kids thought it was cool and it put smiles on their little faces. Anything to make them smile, she thought.

She had contacted Cowboy Al after speaking to her babysitter, Berta. Al was a neighborhood junk collector, and he came by to make her an offer on all the vehicles, plus a few other items standing around. For removal of five old cars plus the roofing shingles left over from building the henhouse and garage, Al offered her one hundred and fifty dollars.

Not much money, but it is a start, she thought as she accepted the deal. He had also wanted the old player piano, but she turned him down cold on that item. Nor could he have the nails, cement, bricks or the lumber laying in the yard, for the house was not done yet. Susan was certain that she and the kids would remain in their country home, and together they would work towards finishing the house.

Another bold decision Susan had made was to take on a boarder who could help out as partial payment for room and board. She thought about this for a long time because the decision would change their household in many ways. The benefits were many: A handyman who could help work on the house and take care of the yard work, another source of income for Susan, perhaps a male role model for the children, and maybe companionship for her.

There were drawbacks as well: Another mouth to feed, another personality thrown into the mix, asking a stranger into their home may not be too smart, and what would happen if Jonathan returns? Susan made her decision in favor of a man named Todd. He seemed safe enough and was arriving on the next Friday. As a framing carpenter for a local home builder, he seemed to be a good choice and met her needs.

Susan was now a waitress at a local diner on Jericho Turnpike, hoarding every penny she earned. She purchased only staple items at the grocery store, such as coffee, milk, juice and butter. The chickens they had were laying eggs daily, and Susan was planning to butcher only one every ten days, making the fresh meat last for as many meals as possible.

Everything had to be stretched out to the utmost, thinning the milk and juice with water to make it last for a week. Catsup was a useful item, and Susan thinned it to make tomato soup and spaghetti sauce. Baking bread was frustrating work for her, but Susan was learning fast and teaching Michelle, now twelve years old and becoming a great little homemaker.

She could take over that responsibility. Indeed, Michelle was now excelling at many of the cooking and cleaning duties, which was a tremendous help to her mother. Berta, Amanda's Swedish Godmother, was happy to care for the children after school and during Susan's shifts at the diner.

She was also instrumental in teaching Michelle how to mend torn clothing and making minor repairs before they became huge issues. Michelle was always happy to sit at the old Singer sewing machine and learn the little tricks that Berta learned as a child in Sweden. She learned skillful ways to hide the flaws while hearing stories of Berta's childhood in the old country.

Afterwards, Michelle would retreat to her bedroom, read her books, and daydream about happier days when Daddy was home, taking the time to play with them. Little Amanda was just so sweet, always smiling and happy. She loved to eat, and Berta was beginning to call her 'Sugar Plumpkin', which Susan was not thrilled about.

It was true though, anytime Amanda began to cry, you only needed to put food in front of her. Her tears would stop, her eyes would light up and she would reach for the snack you were offering. Jennifer was a different story. She was becoming quite a handful, belligerent and disobedient in a variety of ways.

Her schoolwork was suffering and her language was increasingly foul. Each day, Jennifer was returning from school at a very late hour, past dinnertime, and storming up to her room without saying a word. One night Berta made an attempt to address the situation with her but was greeted with a menacing snarl that stopped her right then and there.

This conversation should be handled by Susan, she thought, and she left a detailed note that Jennifer was needing some stern discipline. Berta actually believed that she meant to harm her if she did not step away from her. The girl had really frightened her for a moment, and she was only eight years old!

CHAPTER NINETEEN

Eddie Looks for the Patellis

After Fast Eddy examined the address book he found in the Patelli's house, he decided his first visit would be to the school. Classes would be ending shortly and he wanted to try to pick them up before they got on the bus. Oh boy, Eddy was grinning broadly as he thought about the story he would spin to get those little bastards in the car.

This is right up my alley, he thought. I can lie with the best of them. Just wait 'til I have them in a secluded place! I am gonna have some real fun with those kids – they will never be the same. They will never look at a stranger again without shaking in their boots! Oh yeah! Eddy was sexually excited at the images running through his mind, thinking about the fun he would have with these two kids.

He could not help stroking his hardness as he quickly located the school. Ah, shit. It looks like I missed them. There is not a kid or a school bus in sight. I will have to go into the school office. Still rubbing himself, Eddy struggles with the decision of what to do. Nah, I do not look right for an office visit and they might call the cops. School administrators are a suspicious bunch. Let me just finish up here and I will go on to the next contact.

Several minutes go by and then Eddy is ready to proceed. That really felt good, he thought. Cannot wait to get my hands on that girl! The boy will be ripe, too! I will teach him how to be with a man, and show him how to be with a woman. I wonder which one he will prefer when he grows up.

If Tommy takes him under his wing as I think he will, we will be working together for a long time. A wicked gleam comes into Eddy's eyes as he thinks of where that relationship might go. "Yeah," he says out loud. "Hot damn! Things are just getting better and better!" Ok, let's see. Eddy searches through the address book for the next likely location.

Hmmm. There is an entry here for the mothers' parents under the last name of Stanford. Mom will want to let them know what is going on - women never keep their mouths shut. I will catch up to them over there. The folks live a couple of towns over on the north shore of Oyster Bay in a ritzy neighborhood. I will make sure to return when I have more time to go through that place – people there are loaded and have great stuff in their homes! Especially the ones that live right on the water.

They all have security systems but, hey, it's me, Fast Eddy. He begins to laugh. Yeah, there is not a security system out there that I can't get past! Eddy remembers how many times he used to bet other guys that he was the fastest and the best at breaking through those fancy security systems. After a while, the other guys stopped betting him because they could not win. There is no doubt about it, Fast Eddy is the best!

AT A MOMENT'S NOTICE

Thirty minutes later, Eddy pulls into the Stanford's driveway. During the drive over, he planned how he would approach the parents, but first he needs to know where Sam works. He quickly figures that out from the address book. *This is gonna be really slick*, he thought. He gets out of the car, straightens out his clothes, combs his hair, and calmly walks up to the door.

After ringing the doorbell, he takes a look around through the glass partition, seeing the huge entryway. *These are some really rich people*, he thinks. *Those look like some fine antiques in the entrance.* A few more seconds go by and he rings the bell again. Now he is looking through the window that is nearest to the door. There are lights on but no one is answering the bell. He thinks he hears either a TV or a radio playing.

Eddy decides to walk around to the back of the big fancy house. As he turns the corner, the sounds become louder, and then he walks onto the spacious rear patio where a stereo is playing and a nice looking couple are dancing to the music. Eddy startles them as he approaches, and the woman appears to be very flustered. "Y-yes?" She asks, "We did not hear you ring the bell. Can we help you?"

"Yes ma'am", Eddy responds in his nicest manner. "I am from Telephonics, the same company that Sam Patelli works for. I am sorry to bother you tonight ma'am, but it really is urgent that I reach Sam, and they are not at home tonight. Do you happen to know where they are? I sure would not want Sam to miss out on the new opportunity that just arose, and there is a deadline at eight o'clock tonight."

This gets the man's attention, and he is looking Eddy over pretty closely. "How did you know where to find us?" He asks. Eddy goes out on a limb as he spins his response. "Well, sir, I have known Sam quite a while, and he speaks of you often. In fact, he spoke just recently about the grand holiday party you had; how everyone who was anyone was at your party.

Sam was quite impressed by the guest list and the fine spread you put out. He also admires your home, and that is how I came to know where to find you. As I said, there is this opportunity that came to my attention today but Sam had already left work. He does not answer the phone and he is not at home.

Sam would be just perfect for a position at another location and I wanted to give him a chance to respond before it is too late." Eddy is watching these two, aware that his excuse is flimsy, but hoping to appeal to their good nature with regards to their son-in-law. Now it is time to be quiet and let them decide how to respond.

Eddy calmly stands there without fidgeting, waiting for their answer. The music has stopped and the silence is truly unnerving, but Eddy remains steadfast. After a long minute, the woman intervenes with an answer. "Yes, they have gone away to the mountains for a few days, but I do not know the particulars. I am sorry we could not be more helpful, but that is all we know."

"Thank you very much for your kindness, answers Eddy. I will be going now, enjoy your evening." Eddy quickly returns to the car, leaving the two bewildered people looking at each other. "I do not like it," says the man. "I am calling our neighborhood security to alert them. I need to see his car."

And he walks quickly to the front yard just as Eddy turned out of the driveway. He managed to get a quick look at the car, and thinks it is a dark blue Chevy. The NY license plate begins with DJF, but that is all he got. "Damn. Well, I am calling security anyway. I do not like it," he mutters, as he goes inside to use the phone.

CHAPTER TWENTY

More Hidden Problems

Jonathan is handcuffed to the back door in Officer's Bandeaus' car, and his mind is racing as he looks for a way out of his predicament. The door handle is securely bolted down, so there is no way to get loose. Besides, he did not do anything. If he escapes and runs, the natural assumption is that he is guilty of the murders.

There has to be a way out of this mess! Jonathan wonders if he could explain it to the policeman and satisfy all of his questions, would he be allowed to continue on his way? Would he still be hauled back to NY? The cops will want him to testify in court if they find any suspects, so he is pretty sure he will be heading back to NY again.

No, no, no! I do not want to go back there! I need to find a way out, but I do not want to appear guilty. Then I will be on the run all the time, always looking over my shoulder. What kind of life would that be for Viola? If I return to NY, I will really be in danger from those thugs. They know where I work and probably where my home is as well. There will be no peace for me.

This is like playing a real life Truth or Consequences game, only with dire consequences, Jonathan thinks. I could easily end up dead.

What should I do? At that moment, they pulled into a small gas station and Jonathan makes a snap decision to try a desperate move. He thinks to himself, this is my opportunity. I am not going back.

"Excuse me officer, but my stomach is upset and I really need a bathroom." Jonathan decided he will try to escape from there. "Just wait a minute. I have to check it out first," answers Officer Bandeau. He goes inside to search the bathroom. Good, there is no window. Returning to the car he releases Jonathan from the car handle and escorts him to the men's room, waiting in the small hallway just outside the door.

"Thanks!" responds Jonathan as he steps inside. Now he is quickly looking around for a way to get out. Of course, there is no window. *Damn! Uh, wait a minute now. What is this?* Jon crawls up onto the sink to take a closer look at what appears to be a vent. *Hmm, I wonder if I can get through that small hole?* He takes down the grate using a coin in his pocket, unscrewing the bolts and sticking them in his pocket. A moment later, Officer Bandeau starts knocking on the door. "C'mon, let's go!"

"I am gonna be a couple of minutes - got diarrhea!" Jonathan replies. The grate comes down and looky here - the hole behind the grate is larger than it appeared a moment ago. *I can do this!* thinks Jonathan, and he manages to squeeze in feet first with a little groan, pulling the grate cover behind him. He is able to wedge that cover in place using a matchbook from his pocket. He carefully wiggles back a bit, as far as he can possibly go. He does not want to be seen from the bathroom or from the ground outside. He is actually quite a few feet inside the vent where it is darker than black and feels quite stuffy. He plans to stay here for as long as it takes for that damn cop to give up and go away; hoping that grate stays in place!

The groan was heard by Officer Bandeau, who assumed Jonathan needed another minute due to his diarrhea. Poor guy, his stomach must be really upset with this arrest. But what did he think was going to happen? He is either a witness or an accomplice, and he had to be found. Another minute goes by and Bandeau starts pounding on the door, saying, "I am coming in!" With that, he opens the door to step inside.

"What! Where the fuck did he go!" The bewildered cop is turning around and around and cannot believe that guy got away from him. He runs outside to check the immediate vicinity, but finds no sign of Jonathan. The ground is dry with no muddy areas and there are so many footprints in the area it is impossible to tell what is recent.

There is no window - *how the fuck did he do it?* He scratches his head in complete bewilderment. Richard stood right outside the entire time. Going back inside, he checks the rest stop, asking the station clerk to open up locked areas for him to take a look. The clerk has not seen Jonathan and was no further help to him. Once he is back inside the bathroom he spots the vent up in the ceiling.

Gee, it is awfully small. He could not possibly get through that little hole. Uh huh, there are no screws holding it up. Bandeau runs out to his car to get his flashlight and he borrows a stepstool from the store clerk. Climbing up there, he confirms that the screws have been removed. After pulling down the grate he shines his flashlight into the inky darkness of the vent, slowly flicking the light back and forth.

Jonathan is holding his breath, keeping his face down and hoping that the light will not reveal him. He is thinking about Viola and how surprised she will be when he shows up unannounced. She loves surprises and will be so pleased to see him! Please – do not let that light reveal that I am in here.

CHAPTER TWENTY-ONE

Tommy's Business

Tommy Two Toes is very frustrated now. Just yesterday, Angelo was killed while being punished by Tommy, and that act should have brought great pleasure to him. Today, he sits at the office, pondering his criminal career. He used to take such pride in his savage ability to deal with offenders and incompetent people, but Angelo's death last night has left him feeling unsatisfied.

How could he let that little creep get the better of him, he wonders? And why is he feeling so unsure of himself now? Has he lost his touch, he asks himself? Not being one to reflect inwardly, Tommy is in a very uncomfortable place as he tries to determine why Angelo's death is bothering him, and what to do about it.

As a kid, his dad used to beat the fucking shit out of him if he showed any weakness. His father always told him to be tough. Gary suddenly knocks on Tommy's door and asks, "Hey Boss, what are we doing today? Downstairs is all cleaned up and I am here whenever you need me." Tommy answers him: "Let us go check on some accounts. Some of them are behind and need to pay up."

"Ok Boss," Gary says as he tucks his pistol in his waistband. Did you hear from Eddy yet?" "Nah, says Tommy as they leave the office. I do not expect to hear from him until his job on the Parelli family is completed. That oughta be some story since it is taking him so damn long. I expected him back here yesterday."

The two men drive off in Tommy's brand new Cadillac Eldorado Brougham. It was the first year of this particular Cadillac and Tommy was very proud of his new acquisition that set him back a whopping thirteen thousand dollars - a small fortune in 1957! There were unbelievable new features, such as cruise control and electric locks, which Tommy liked to brag about.

It was a gleaming burgundy color with a brushed stainless steel roof and white leather interior, complete with a stereo music system. The beautiful new car was Tommy's pride and joy. He even named this beauty Lola, but he did not mention it to his wife. He did not want her to be jealous.

Tommy's insecurities fade away during the normal course of business in the next few hours. He enjoys teaching Gary how to collect funds owed for the protection that Tommy provides. That protection is from the mobsters of other territories who occasionally try to steal entire blocks away from Tommy. Tommy's territory has expanded considerably over the past couple of years and he is good at keeping his merchants in line.

Gary proves himself as a reliable and competent account collector as the two men make their rounds. Gary shows each merchant the menacing side of his personality to let them know he is not to be trifled with. It is 'Pay up and shut up' with Gary in control, and Tommy really likes that.

This guy is a natural gangster, Tommy thinks. *All he needs is some guidance, and he will be my next in command. He might be too smart, though. I will need to keep him under control so he does not think he can get the jump on me. Still, I am glad to have him on my team. Eddy is a great right-hand-man, but he is not a born leader like Gary seems to be.*

Eddy does as he is told. Gary takes initiative. Both men excel at their work, each one in their own capacity. Tommy is lucky to have them and works hard at keeping them happy and keeping them in their place. He does not want them to get too big for their britches and try to take over the business.

After several hours, the men wrap up their work and are heading back to the Cadillac. Suddenly, Tommy stops short, his jaw drops and he stands there in disbelief. All of a sudden, he begins screaming a string of profanities as he lunges toward his new car and looks at the malicious and intentional damage. "Who the fuck did this!" he screams, as he turns around and around, looking for the culprit.

"I – I – I cannot believe this shit!" The windshield was smashed in, as were the lights all around the car. Something sharp was used to scrape "Killer" on one side of the car and "Burn in Hell" on the other side. "Watch your back" was etched into the hood of the once beautiful car. Tommy stood there for a moment with his head hung, as if a knife went through his heart. His beautiful Lola had been ruined. Gary was immediately on the alert, gun drawn and hunkered down.

He tried to drag Tommy down with him as he scanned the area for the guy responsible for such unimaginable destruction, but Tommy was now in an uncontrollable rage. His eyes were glazed over and crazy. He was looking everywhere, searching for the guy who did this unspeakable act.

After another minute of struggling with him, Gary was able to shove Tommy into the back seat and they drove off in the direction of Tommy's office. Gary saw Tommy's furious rage was out of control, and thought, somebody is gonna pay.

CHAPTER TWENTY-TWO

NYPD Case Status

Chief Walter Hadley of the New York City Police Department was beginning to take heat from the mayor's office because the Pratel murder case was at a standstill. It had been almost a week since the high profile murders were committed at Marty's Garage in downtown Manhattan, and they had no concrete leads left.

They were no closer to apprehending a suspect now than they were the day after it happened. The mayor was demanding something that would show progress from Chief Hadley, who now felt like an imbecile. Officer Bandeau was out on a personal leave of absence, which really annoyed Chief Hadley because he was the first responder at the scene.

What was he thinking, to leave at a time like this? Why would he do that? Is it possible that Bandeau had more information on this case and took off to follow his own leads? Everyone's help was needed as the two investigators on the case were at a dead end with no more leads to follow. Bandeau and I will be discussing this as soon as he returns, the Chief promised himself. *I cannot permit any loose cannons to be allowed to run around on their own.*

His leave of absence better be for sickness or personal reasons. Otherwise, I will have to discipline him to set an example for the team. Family members of the two victims were questioned on several occasions for possible motives and connections, but that yielded no further information. Another possible connection was the wife of the parking garage manager, who actually witnessed the murders.

Chief Hadley finds it strange that the witness has just disappeared off the face of the earth. Either the killer found him and disposed of him already, or he is on the run and afraid to return home. He is out there somewhere, he could feel it in his gut. According to the two officers who interviewed her, the wife was a bundle of nerves, worried about her husband and children.

The only information she offered was that her husband had a girlfriend in the city someplace, but unfortunately, she did not know the girlfriend's location. Jonathan's notebook was found on the garage floor, which contained several pages of handwritten remarks, including names and phone numbers of several unknown people.

Each person was contacted but they were all private customers of his - apparently the man worked on the side as a handyman. Again, no leads were discovered. The tire tracks left in the dirt inside the garage simply gave the brand and model of the getaway car's tires, which happened to be very common.

The bullet casings found on the garage floor did have identifiable markings on them, but they did not match up with anything that was on record. No good leads could be gleaned from these clues. Chief Hadley was frustrated and pacing around his office, like a caged lion. He was ready to bite off the head of the next person who walked into his office.

Everything seemed to lead to a dead end. This is the kind of case that makes or breaks careers, he thought. *If I do not solve this case,* it will most likely mean no re-appointment next year. What have I missed? There has to be something concrete that will lead to the murderer. He finally sits down and scrutinizes the file once again.

An hour later, Chief Hadley picks up his phone to call the Chief Investigator, David Sperl. "Sperl", answers the investigator. Chief Hadley barks into the phone, "I am calling an early morning meeting of all investigators and officers working on this Pratel case. I want to see everyone in my office at 0600 tomorrow - no exceptions! All information, notes, details should be in hand. Got that?"

"Yes sir!" responds Investigator Sperl. "Good! Get it done!" says Chief Hadley, slamming down the phone while a gnawing pain starts working in his stomach. I know we have missed something, and tomorrow we are not leaving this office until we find it, dammit! vows Chief Hadley.

CHAPTER TWENTY-THREE

Resistance

Susan has made a lot of adjustments in the short time that Jonathan has been missing. She has come to the conclusion that she might never see him again, although she still keeps the children hopeful. It breaks her heart, but Susan continues to remind them of fun outings they had as a family, special times they enjoyed with their father, and how good he always was to them.

She was the disciplinarian. He never scolded or disciplined them for mistakes they made. Jonathan's response to that stuff was usually a chuckle, "Oops!" being the most he said. Jonathan is just a big, happy-go-lucky kid. In the meantime, Susan has been working two part-time jobs.

Susan is still a waitress at the local diner, plus, she found a temporary position as a hostess in a posh restaurant. She finds the work enjoyable and is saving her money the entire spring while she has this job. They will not need her services over the summer months, and they will take her back in the fall season if she does a good job now.

The patrons like her so she feels confident that she will receive the job offer again in September. The extra money is being spent on food and building supplies for the house. It is just as well to have some free time in the summer for the kids. They have been through so much and it is not fair that I work all the time.

That is like losing both parents, and she needs to keep them on the right track, thinks Susan. They need her attention and to feel loved more than ever. Jennifer has already been the cause of trouble, as reported by the babysitter. Susan was horrified to hear that Jennifer threatened Berta, and she was crying as Berta told her the details of that night.

The next day after Jennifer went to school - or appeared to go to school - Susan went through every nook and cranny of Jennifer's bedroom. She is really dismayed at all the cash she found tucked into her socks in the underwear drawer. *How could this be? Where did she get all this money? My goodness, there is almost one hundred dollars here!* It is incredible to see all these five and ten dollar bills! *One hundred dollars! I would have to work a month for that kind of money! What the heck could an eight year old be getting into?*

She is going to have a stern talk with Jennifer and issue some discipline. Susan plans to ground her from all outside activities for a month and give her extra duties at home during that time. For crying out loud, Jennifer is only eight years old and she threatened her babysitter! Susan could just wrap her hands around her throat, she is so frustrated with that girl. And what about the money? *I should ground her for life! I do not need this on top of everything else, she mumbles to herself.*

Her grades at school are slipping as well, so she will be contacting her teacher. Jennifer is a smart girl and was a model student until Jonathan disappeared. Susan is afraid of losing her grip on her daughter. She has been unusually quiet and appears to be angry most of the time. She will not be surprised if the teacher reports that she is absent from class a lot.

She realizes that a visit for Jennifer to see the school psychologist would also be time well spent, and makes a note to do that when she sees the teacher. Tomorrow is Tuesday and she will make those appointments to get in to school as soon as possible. Where does she go? Who is she with? What is she doing? What kind of trouble is she causing, or finding?

There are a million ways Jennifer's life could be drastically altered by being in the wrong place at the wrong time. I will do my very best to straighten her out now, vows Susan. I just cannot let Jennifer slip through my fingers! I am going to sit Jennifer down today after school and get to the bottom of this. I need to know what the heck is going on!

Well, she thinks, I did one thing right when I offered room and board to Todd. That man has certainly been a big help. The first thing he did was build his own little bedroom onto the back porch. It did not take him long to do it and he moved right in. His carpentry, electrical and plumbing skills are extensive and he will be a reliable worker to help Susan finish building the house.

Since he is a local framing carpenter, Todd will probably have some spare time during poor weather, and he can spend that time working on projects at home. Todd does not hesitate to pitch in and help wherever needed, even if it is just washing dishes. The low rent he pays Susan is being stashed away in a savings account. Susan does not ever want to feel destitute again.

She wants to know there will be money available when she needs it. In addition, his carpentry skills are a huge help in finishing the house. Unfortunately, Todd and the children are not getting along. She was hoping he would provide a male role model, but perhaps it is too soon for that to happen.

The two older kids are feeling as if Todd is there to replace their dad, although Susan has assured them repeatedly that is not true. Todd is there to lend his help because they desperately need it. Only little Amanda accepts his presence with a smile.

CHAPTER TWENTY-FOUR

Protection

The Patelli family left their home within ten minutes of the arrival of Sargents Whitfield and Belafonte. Two cars were used, with Sam and Tommy in the lead car with Sargent Whitfield, and Carolyn and Wanda following with Sargent Belafonte. The officers were taking them to a safe house far north in the Finger Lakes area of New York; the drive would take several hours.

During the long drive, the children were entertained with fun road trip games like cribbage and car bingo to keep their attention diverted from the underlying current of fear possessed by their parents. The officers were enjoying the delight of the children, even though they were on the lookout for possible signs of trouble from the mob.

Sam and Carolyn began to relax once they were well past New York City. The miles seemed to melt away their anxiety and they were calming down, beginning to feel safe. After about six hours, the group arrived at their destination without incident. The hideaway was a luxury vacation cabin owned by a friend of Chief Hadley, and occasionally rented by the police department as a safe house.

There were four bedrooms, each with a fireplace, three bathrooms, living room and den, also with a fireplace, and a spacious kitchen with plenty of room for everyone. Just outside the kitchen door was a huge stack of ready-cut firewood. The place was self-contained, well stocked with food and supplies for several weeks.

The garage had several secure gun cabinets with enough firepower for a small army, plus, there was a reinforced safe room located beneath the house with additional weapons, food and water.

The cabin was tucked away in the deep woods with a large clearing surrounding the house. They would have a clear line of sight in all directions, should anyone try to approach the cabin. "Wow!" was the general consensus of the group as they entered their temporary accommodations.

Tommy and Wanda immediately ran upstairs to claim their bedrooms, which left Sam and Carolyn smiling in gratitude. "Would you like me to put on coffee? Carolyn asks the officers. It looks like I could make you some breakfast or light dinner, the kitchen is already stocked with food."

"Just coffee please", the officers answer simultaneously. Sargent Belafonte says, "We will get ourselves set up, here. Please remember to stay inside the house at all times, and stay away from the windows. We do not expect any trouble out here, but you never know. We must take precautions. Sargent Benny Whitfield will take first watch. One of us will always be watching," says Sargent Henry Belafonte.

"Yes," says Sargent Whitfield. "The children also need to stay within the boundaries we have explained. Please see that they understand. There is to be no outside activity - I know they will be itching to get out in the snow, but they must stay inside. You will see to that, right Carolyn?"

"Yes, of course, Sargent Whitfield," she answers. "Sam, please come with me. I would like to explain our plan of action here so you will not be taken by surprise." With that said, Sam follows Sargent Belafonte into the garage area where a chalkboard is set up. The officer begins to sketch diagrams of the property on the chalkboard, indicating entry and exit points to both the interior of the house and the exterior property.

He is slowly explaining to Sam just what kind of action to take in the event of many different scenarios. Each one is very detailed. Henry is trying to cover all the angles; anything that might come up. With every situation, the officer stops to ask if Sam understands. At the end, he studies Sam for a moment, then says, "Sam, this is a serious predicament and we all need to be careful.

There can be no errors. A mistake could cost someone their life, and we need to be sharp about this stuff. You are going to study this board until you can draw it in your sleep.

Tomorrow, the entire family will be taken through some practice drills, plus I will be quizzing you on these sketches in the evening. I want to give you some time to assimilate this information. It has to become a part of you.

You will be their leader; I am counting on you to keep your family under control while Benny and I take care of the perpetrators if they arrive. Is that clear?" Sam is looking a bit dazed, but nods 'yes' in compliance. He is tired from the long trip, but he will do a better job of grasping all this detailed information tomorrow.

Practice drills for the family - the kids will love it! Plus a quiz for him - oh brother! So far there has been no sign of any dangerous element, and for now they just need to pray for a safe night in their new place. After Sam goes to bed that night he is thinking about the sketches, when suddenly he hears a loud crash!

Jumping out of bed and scaring Carolyn half to death, Sam goes charging downstairs. Sargent Whitfield hears the commotion and grabs Sam at the foot of the staircase. "Whoa!" says the officer. What is wrong?" "I heard a crashing sound - like someone coming through a window! Did you hear it?" replies Sam.

"There is no one here, Sam. No one has entered the house and no window has been broken," replies Sargent Whitfield. "Would you like to join me for a premise check? We will go check it out." "Ok," says Sam as they begin to check the entire house, room by room. "But I am certain I heard breaking glass."

Ten minutes later, Sam looks sheepishly at the officer and says, "I really thought I heard someone breaking in, but I guess it was just a dream. Sorry I bothered you." "It is no trouble; that is what we are here for. Go back to bed and try to relax – we have you covered." The officer resumes his patrol and Sam joins his restless wife for a night of uneasy sleep.

CHAPTER TWENTY-FIVE

The Big Fancy House

Eddy's search for the Patelli's has stalled for now. His mind is racing with possibilities as to where they fled, but "gone to the mountains for a vacation," as described by Sam Patelli's mother, is pretty thin. In this area of the country that could be just about anywhere, like in New York or Pennsylvania, for starters.

He thoroughly searched their address book - his only resource from the Patelli house - and there is no indication that they own a mountain home. When Eddy reached out to his best informer, Mac McKnight, he asked him to connect with the NYPD and find out if the Patelli's have been relocated for their protection. That is the only thing that makes sense.

They are gonna need plenty of protection, alright, thinks Eddy. *This is only making it worse for them. The harder they make me work to find 'em, the more I am gonna make 'em pay.* "Just you wait!" he starts yelling out loud. "I am gonna find you and tear you apart! No one gets one over on Fast Eddy!"

Eddy glances over at the driver of the car next to him and begins to calm down a bit. He forgot that he was driving with the window open.

That driver is looking him over pretty closely, having heard all the commotion. Eddy gives him a goofy smile and a shrug before driving on ahead.

I cannot afford to have any extra attention on me tonight because I am going back to that big, fancy house in Oyster Bay. If I cannot report back to Tommy with positive news about the Parelli's, maybe I can please him with some extraordinary pieces from Oyster Bay. I cannot wait to see what they have in there! I am gonna make sure I get a big haul from that house - I bet it is loaded with good stuff!

Meanwhile, Mac will work his magic at the Police Department and get back to me with info about the Parelli's. I will continue my search for the Patelli's when I hear from him. Yeah, maybe I can do both jobs and really make Tommy proud of me. Eddy works his way slowly back to the Oyster Bay house, taking his time, because the place will most likely be occupied by the owners.

The most dangerous burglaries are done with people in the residence. He has done it successfully once before. That job was especially worthwhile, as he discovered a major cache of very old silver coins dating back to the 1800's. Tommy was laughing with glee when Eddy presented his find.

What will he find tonight, he wonders, rubbing his hands together in anticipation. He already knows there are antiques in the house. These people are collectors of valuable items. He is looking for small items of value like silver and gold, precious jewelry, cash, bearer bonds - anything like that.

Then he will inform one of his friends who specialize in the larger items, such as art work and antique furniture – they will be able to fence whatever they take, giving him a handsome finder's fee for passing along the information. *Ah, life is sweet*, he thinks. *Ok, it is after midnight and the owners should be asleep by now*, Eddy thinks, as he drives through the open gates of the exclusive neighborhood. "Let's get this done", he says to himself.

Unknown to Eddy, the security guard was watching him from the dark confines of his parked car as Eddy entered the quiet community. He had the description given to him earlier by the homeowner, and this car was a perfect match. He quickly entered the security booth and phoned the local police.

He passed along the complete description and the address involved, alerting the officer of all the details from earlier. "We are on our way," answered the officer. The security guard drives around to the address involved, parking several houses away on the opposite side of the street. He witnesses Eddy as he deftly enters the house through a side window after quickly disabling the security alarm.

This guy is good, he is thinking. He did that so fast! It will be good to catch this guy *and put him out of commission. The cops should be here any second.* Once inside, Eddy quietly gets his bearings within the semi darkened house. *I am glad they leave lights on for added security*, he chuckles to himself. *This way I can see where I am going and make my hit even faster!*

Ok, this is a formal dining room. I bet they have sterling silverware, he thinks, as he begins going through the breakfront cabinet. *Yep, here it is. Man, they have a shitload of silver here!* Eddy takes two large cloth tablecloths and wraps up all the silverware he can find, being careful not to make any noise. He also sees larger silver serving pieces and makes a mental note to pass that info along to his friend.

Going back to the window he entered through, Eddy leaves his find on the floor and continues to search the house. He is looking for either a den or an office, both of which he finds. In the den, Eddy discovers more antique furniture, which he will pass along. He now focuses on the office, hoping to find cash and other valuables.

Eddy is not disappointed! He locates a floor safe under the desk and quickly gains access, laughing to himself about the gullibility of most rich people who believe their stuff is secure in the store bought safes they use. "Look-it this stuff! I have hit the jackpot!

Silver and gold coins, gold bullion, exquisite diamond jewelry, and stacks of cash! This is Nirvana!" Eddy envisions Tommy's reaction as he scoops everything into the extra tablecloth he brought along from the dining room.

Going back to the access window now, Eddy knows it is time for him to go. He has been here long enough and has made quite a nice haul! The folks upstairs never heard a sound - won't they be surprised when they wake up tomorrow. He carefully lowers the three bundles of loot through the open window and down to the ground before climbing out himself, only to be met by two uniformed police officers.

"That is far enough! Hands up and do not move!" the officers bark at him as they train their spotlight on him now. Guns are drawn and they cautiously approach Eddy as his heart sinks. *Ah, fuck it all!* Thinks Eddy. There will be no getting out of this, and when Tommy finds out, Eddy will be really screwed!

CHAPTER TWENTY-SIX

The Road to Change

Although it has only been about thirty minutes, to Jonathan it feels like he has been inside the small vent for a very long time. So far, he has not been discovered and he is beginning to think he fooled the cop. *I will wait just a bit longer*, Jon thinks to himself. I want to be sure the officer has given up and gone away.

He is actually starting to feel sleepy and does not see any harm in taking a little nap. He is feeling confident that the cop was not coming back here to look again - and was probably still searching the nearby woods. With that, Jonathan closed his eyes and drifted off to sleep. Meanwhile, Officer Bandeau has been going nuts trying to figure out what happened to his prisoner.

What happened to him? There is absolutely no sign of him - he disappeared into thin air! Where the Hell did he go? He began to look again through the small wooded area to be sure he was not tucked away in the bushes. He was glad that he never told anyone in New York about coming out here to find the guy! *How embarrassing it would be to have this happen to me!* The guy clearly outsmarted Officer Bandeau and he was infuriated.

After another twenty minutes of looking through the woods, Officer Bandeau thought, *I bet he went back to his truck so he could continue on his way out west. I am going back to the truck to wait for him to show up. I can hide out in the woods and grab him when he returns - and this time, I am not falling for any of his nonsense!*

Bandeau gets in his car and does exactly that - he goes back to the wooded area to wait for Jonathan to arrive. While he waits he continues to soothe his wounded ego by thinking of how he will treat Jonathan once he has him in custody. *No more Mister Nice Guy!* Jonathan has to pay for making him feel stupid. *He will remember this for a long time,* thinks Bandeau.

About an hour later, Jonathan wakes up and decides it is safe to come out of the tiny vent where he has been hiding. He is very stiff from laying in that cramped little vent and carefully climbs down from his perch up in the wall. "Aaah, it feels good to stretch out, not to mention, get some fresh air", he says to himself. *I cannot believe this worked,* he is thinking.

I got lucky! "That cop must be feeling pretty stupid", Jonathan is chuckling now. Jonathan knows exactly what he is going to do now. He had plenty of time to think it through while he was waiting for time to pass. He quietly leaves the gas station - he does not want the clerk to see him leave. *I am not taking any chances that the police might be alerted,* he thinks.

He still plans to go out west to California, but he is not going back to pick up his truck. That vehicle is much too hot now; the police will be watching for his return. Heading out at a run, Jonathan is going to the nearest highway. He plans to flag down a truck driver and hitch a ride. By doing this, his journey will not be as direct and will not be traceable, either. *The cops will not find him again,* he vows to himself.

He reaches the highway in about half an hour and it is busy with traffic. It did not take long for Jonathan to pick up a ride with a truck going to Boseman, Montana. *That is perfect*, he thought. *No one will be looking for me on the highway to Boseman, and maybe I will rest for a day or so while I am there.*

I want to think things through a little more before I reach Viola's place. I cannot wait to see her. It would be best if I had a plan to offer her when I show up. I can clean myself up a bit, too. I have not seen Viola for a long time and I want to make a good impression on her, even if I am on the lam.

Viola, I am coming home, honey - was his last thought as he drifted asleep in the cab of the truck going to Montana. Jonathan was so exhausted he fell deep asleep, lulled by the whine of the tires on the pavement and the rocking motion of the cab. He was completely oblivious to the sounds of the traffic and the CB radio used by the trucker.

He never heard the CB chatter between several truckers who were relaying information about the road blocks ahead in Fargo, North Dakota. Apparently, the Troopers were looking for a dangerous murderer and all vehicles were being searched at the North Dakota/Minnesota border. *Were they looking for the guy sleeping next to him*, the truck driver wondered, as he looked over at Jonathan?

CHAPTER TWENTY-SEVEN

Jennifer, Where Are You?

Susan spent the night worrying about her daughter, Jennifer. She had returned home late last night and stormed up to her room without saying a word to anyone. Susan had followed her upstairs, but was unable to talk to her. "Jennifer, I need to speak to you," Susan had said to her. Jennifer refused to speak to her, slamming the door to her bedroom in her face!

When she tried to open the door, Susan discovered, to her amazement, that it was locked! *This door never had a lock,* she thought, he must have put it on himself. How does an eight year old do that? "Jennifer, what have you gotten yourself into?" she said to herself, beginning to feel apprehensive. She decided to leave her alone - for now.

In the early morning, after a sleepless night, Susan went to Jennifer's room to wake her up and see if she would talk to her. Maybe they could have breakfast together. To her shock, she discovers the room is vacant, and the money she had found in her sock drawer a few days ago is gone. As she looks around her room, she notices that her duffel bag and some of her clothes are gone!

AT A MOMENT'S NOTICE

"Oh my god! Where the Hell has she gone?" She whispers, afraid of what this might mean. "Jennifer, what are you doing? What have you gotten yourself into?" a nervous feeling building up inside her. Jennifer was a smart girl, and had that same impatient ambition like her dad. What could she be up to?

With the nervous pit in her stomach getting bigger and heavier, Susan went into the living room to call the police - she was going to report Jennifer as missing. While waiting for the officer to arrive, Susan gets Amanda ready for her babysitter and sends Michele off to school. Just before getting herself ready for work, there is a loud knock on the door.

Going downstairs, she looked out the window to see who was knocking. Standing there on her porch, is a rather large young man in his twenties, kind of seedy looking with long blonde hair, a scruffy beard and tattoos on both arms. Susan takes a step back and says, "Yes?"

"Jennifer live here?" he asks in a gruff manner. "Who wants to know?" she asks in an equally gruff manner. "Name's Bill", he answers. "Jennifer has something that belongs to me and I come to get it." To Susan's relief, a patrol car pulls up right then. "You can explain it all to him", Susan gestures at the police car. However, the seedy young man is already running through the back yard.

The police officer witnessed this and immediately takes off after him, catching up to him three yards over and hauling him back to Susan's house. "Ma'am, I am Officer Carlisle. You called regarding a missing child? Does this fellow have anything to do with that?" "Yes, I believe so", responds Susan. "This man just arrived and he was asking to see my daughter, Jennifer.

Jennifer is the child that is missing since yesterday. I have no idea who this guy is or what he has to do with my child, but Jennifer left home sometime last night and I do not know where she went." Officer Carlisle herds everyone into the living room and begins his questioning with the young man, named Bill. "Do you have any identification on you?"

"Yeah, here is my driver's license", answers Bill as he hands it to the cop. Next, Officer Carlisle asks, "How do you know Jennifer and what exactly is it you want with her?" Bill begins to squirm around in his chair. "Uh, well now, Jennifer has some money of mine. I gave it to her to hold last week, and I told her I would be picking it up today."

"Really", says the skeptical officer. "How much money, where did you get it, and why in the world would you give it to an eight-year-old-kid to hold onto?" Susan is sitting close by on pins and needles, chewing on her fingernails, watching the exchange between the two men. She is anxious about the location of her young daughter, but does not interrupt the interrogation, knowing that eventually the officer will try to get Jennifer's location out of Bill.

Bill replies slowly, choosing his words with care, "It was only one hundred dollars, and the money was given to her as a test. I wanted to see if she could be trusted. Jennifer knew the money had to be returned to me - the full amount, today." "Just why do you need to trust an eight year old with money?" asks the officer.

"Uh, well, um", responds Bill. "She was gonna do me a favor every week and pick something up for me." "So, where is Jennifer now? Why is she not here to pay you?" asks the officer. Bill's response was nasty: "How the fuck do I know? Kid's s'posed to be here with my money."

The officer ignores Bill and his comment for now and turns to Susan to take a full report on her missing child. He is very careful to note all the details given to him by Susan and gets a recent photo of the girl from her. "Your daughter will most likely return home today, in which case you must notify Police Headquarters immediately.

If you do not hear from her by tomorrow, call me at the number listed on this business card." He says, as he hands her his card. Susan is keeping herself together emotionally, but just barely. She keeps glancing at Bill, who appears very calm and uncaring. Susan hates this creep who has obviously involved her child in some kind of illegal activity.

At this point, Officer Carlisle stands up to handcuff Bill, telling him that they are going down to the police station and that Bill could possibly be implicated in the disappearance of Jennifer, among other things. As Officer Carlisle and a handcuffed Bill leave in the patrol car, Susan bursts into uncontrollable sobs. *Jennifer, where are you?* She thinks, as she wipes her tears, "Please, just come home!"

CHAPTER TWENTY-EIGHT

The Worst Kind of Death

As Gary drove them back to Tommy's office, Tommy was in an absolute rage in the backseat of the ruined Cadillac. After several minutes of cursing and pounding on the back of the front seat, Tommy stopped to take a few deep breaths. They were pulling into his garage at the office, and Tommy looked Gary squarely in the eyes.

"Whoever did this to my Lola will never get away with it." he said with a cold calm that made Gary squirm. "I will hunt them down. Those motherfuckers will not escape. They will pay with their very lives. No one treats Tommy Two Toes like this," he said, with a terrifying look on his face.

With that said, Tommy goes inside to have dinner with his wife, Lucinda, and Gary heads into the office to make his journal entries for Tommy, thinking about how much Hell this man can dish out. Who could have gotten the leg up on Tommy? He thought about how he could assist Tommy with his search for the lowlife culprit who tore up Tommy's Cadillac, fondly nicknamed, Lola.

To keep his top ranking, Gary needs to keep proving himself to the boss, making his services become indispensable. Finding out who is responsible for this catastrophe will go a long way to becoming Tommy's new right-hand-man, especially with Fast Eddy out of the way for a few days.

Suddenly, he hears some very loud, horrific sounds coming from Tommy's home. There is a loud crash and blood-curdling screams! "What the Hell?" Gary shouts. Gary goes running to the front door of the apartment and barges right in without knocking. He stops immediately, horrified at the scene before him.

There is broken glass just inside the doorway, and the couch has been shredded. There is blood everywhere! *Oh my God! What happened? Is Tommy ok?* Gary sees that the place has been thoroughly ransacked. Whose blood is it? *Oh dear God, is that Lucinda's arm? What happened here?*

He walks slowly from room to room without touching anything, to survey the damage, and then he finds Tommy holding Lucinda, rocking back and forth. Tommy is screaming at the top of his lungs, "No! Oh God, No! My baby! Who did this to my baby! I'll kill 'em! I'll fucking kill 'em!" Now Tommy collapses onto the floor, face down on his knees, sobbing and moaning next to his dead Lucinda.

As Gary takes in the scene, he thinks this is the worst kind of death imaginable for such a lovely lady. And she was a lady, untouched by Tommy's cruel and brutal business. Lucinda never got involved, never asked questions or demanded answers. She loved Tommy despite his business and never wanted to know about that side of him. Who could do this to such a gentle soul?

"Ok, Tommy", he says, firmly touching the mobster's shoulder. "C'mon now, get up. Let's get you outta here." Gary thinks they should call the cops but he knows that Tommy will not do that. Tommy will take care of this nasty business in his own manner. But first, the place needs to be cleaned up.

Gary takes a closer look at her body, which is lying on the cold kitchen floor. He sees the butcher knife in her right hand and the meat cleaver lying close by on the counter. Her left forearm is missing - he had seen it laying in the living room, drained of blood. Lucinda's body is badly cut up with very deep gashes across her torso.

It looks like she was attacked with the meat cleaver and she was trying to protect herself with the butcher knife. Half of her once lovely face was sliced away, making her look particularly gruesome. The blood is already congealed, brown and sticky, leading Gary to believe this happened several hours ago.

He wonders if anything was stolen, and will ask Tommy after he calms down a bit. First, he needs to get Tommy to a safe place. This is obviously an act of revenge, targeting Tommy and all that he loves. Both the car and his wife were his "trophies"; his most cherished "possessions".

Gary turns his attention back to Tommy. "C'mon, let's go now. We will take a ride to my place for a while." Gary makes sure both the residence and the office are secured before they leave. Tommy's head is hanging low, his shoulders are stooped and he is shuffling along as Gary puts him in his Ford Thunderbird, preferring not to use the Cadillac, which will only give away their location.

Gary's apartment is just a few blocks away and they arrive without incident. Tommy is completely dazed and follows Gary's instructions without comment, without even looking up at Gary. They go inside together and Gary gets Tommy a stiff drink of whiskey, settling him down on the couch. Tommy is staring into his drink. Just staring.

After a minute, he looks at Gary and says, "She is gone?" He stares back at his drink for another minute. Gary does not answer but places his hand on Tommy's shoulder. "Yeah," Tommy says. "She is gone.

Lucinda is the only one I ever loved. Lucinda was so special, and I loved her. What will I do now? What will I do without Lucinda?" Tommy lapses into soft crying, looking into his drink. Gary sighs and picks up the phone to make a call.

CHAPTER TWENTY-NINE

Priorities

Their first night at the luxurious mountain cabin was very exciting for the Patelli children. They could not wait until the next day to check out the cabin, so they spent a couple of excited hours, running to and fro, having fun while they check out every nook and cranny. Then, Wanda and Tommy fell deep asleep in their bedrooms without feeling a moment's anxiety.

Sam and Carolyn went to bed soon after the children, but sleep did not come so easily to them. They knew that a criminal was searching for them, planning to destroy their happy family because Sam had witnessed a brutal crime several months ago and had taken steps to testify in court against the mobster, Tommy Two Toes.

Sam was not aware that a similar thing happened to Jonathan, who was running from Tommy Two Toes and his thugs. Meanwhile, a police officer was on duty, patrolling the hallways, checking doors and windows. After six hours on duty, the other officer picked up the patrol so the first one could get some rest.

In the morning, they had a full day of survivor training scheduled for the family to learn how they could be helpful in the event the uninvited visitors with guns showed up. The next day, everyone woke up to a fresh snowfall on the ground and a bright, sunny day. As the officers' predicted, the kids wanted to rush outside to play in the snow, but Carolyn did a great job of distracting them with indoor activities until it was time for the officers to begin their training.

Sargent Benny Whitfield was in charge of training the children, and they began to practice at ten AM. The kids were all giggles as they marched up and down the hallways, learning how to patrol each individual room and check doors and windows. After a short break at ten thirty, Benny taught them how to enter a room cautiously, scanning the room before entering it to check the doors and windows.

Now the kids were getting the feeling that this was a serious issue, and the giggles faded away. At eleven fifteen, Benny had Tommy and Wanda follow him through several mock escape routes. If an intruder entered through the garage, they were trained to follow route number one that led them out of the house through the back door.

If someone entered through the front door, they would follow route number two, going out the side door. There was a route developed for each scenario that the children had to learn before lunch. After lunch, Benny tested Tommy and Wanda by pretending to be the bad guy and watching how the two responded.

Tommy was clearly the leader in this exercise, often looking out for his sister and leading her down the correct route to safety. By three o'clock PM, Benny was satisfied with the results and gave both kids a gold star for the day. The children were now free to watch television or play indoor games, but there was no outdoor activity permitted.

While the children were doing their practice drills, Sargent Henry Belafonte had Carolyn and Sam in the garage learning the routes that the children were being taught. The scenario drawn on the chalkboard was changed again and again, and the parents were being quizzed on each sketch until Henry was happy that they knew the routes.

Next, he taught them how to evade the intruders if both the officers were removed from the picture, how they should call for help, and where they should seek refuge until help arrived. These last few lessons were the most critical ones and Henry spent a lot of time going over them.

At three PM, he was finished with the parents, asking them to gather as a family in the den at seven PM. The family was going to run through a practice drill as a group, at least once before bedtime. Of course, the kids thought this was a great new game, not realizing the danger they potentially faced.

The parents were feeling better prepared, but still terrified, because they were completely aware of their predicament. They were so grateful to the New York City Police Department for the pains taken on their behalf. Henry and Benny had to be two of the nicest officers; well trained and very skilled for the job at hand. Still, the parents were stressed and fearful for their lives.

Just before seven o'clock, Henry heard an unusual sound coming from the rear of the house, near the children's bedrooms. As he quietly ran to investigate, he silently signaled to Sam to get the family under wraps in the basement safe room. Sam did this without hesitation, locking his family into this specially designed soundproof room with newly developed TV cameras that allowed them to watch from within, but no one could see them inside.

Benny ran upstairs to flank his partner, who was secretly watching an intruder break in through Wanda's bedroom window. From the looks of this intruder, it was impossible to believe that this guy was any kind of gangster. He was fumbling about, making unnecessary noise, and even dropped his toolkit at one point.

What an idiot, thought Henry, as the two officers stepped out to confront this burglar with their weapons drawn. Clearly startled by the sudden appearance of the policemen, the burglar immediately resigned himself to capture. He bashfully answered all questions posed by the officers who knew this had to be his first attempt at becoming a criminal.

Henry placed a call to the local police department, asking them to send a unit to pick up the would-be thief. When that unit arrived, it was disclosed to Benny and Henry that the intruder was really an undercover cop who had been instructed to "break-in" for a real-life practice drill, but don't be difficult to catch. That information would not be disclosed to the Patelli's.

Once the intruder was removed from the premises, Benny returned to the safe room and retrieved the family from their hiding place. "Ok, that is enough for today. Great job everyone! You knew just what to do. You guys get some sleep now and we will practice again tomorrow. I have the first watch, so do not worry. One of us will always be on patrol."

Carolyn put both children to bed in Tommy's room, since Wanda's room now had a broken window. By the time she got them settled down and had read them a soothing story to calm their excitement, Henry already had a wooden board nailed up over the broken window and he tightly sealed the door shut with bedding to keep out any cold draft.

Once Carolyn and Sam were huddled together in bed trying to get warm, they began to discuss this newest event. "What else will we be faced with!?" exclaimed Carolyn. "It is kind of hard to believe that this was an isolated incident" was Sam's comment. He did not know that this was a staged burglary.

This incident really heightened their awareness. Neither of them could calm down and Carolyn was trembling uncontrollably while Sam tried to massage away her fears. It was not working. Eventually, they both drifted off into a fitful sleep, filled with trepidation about tomorrow.

CHAPTER THIRTY

Failure

Fast Eddy knew when he was caught red-handed in a burglary attempt on Long Island that there would be Hell to pay, and then some. For the first time, he was scared. First of all, he failed to resolve the Patelli situation for Tommy Two Toes. He still had no idea where those two disappeared to with their family.

His job was to dispose of the entire family - and he could not even find them! Where the Hell were they? With him being locked up, there was no way to finish the job assigned to him by Tommy. The Patelli's really got one over on him, and Eddy was pissed off! Second, his arrest would ultimately lead to implicating Tommy.

Their careers were too intertwined for that fact to be missed. Tommy and Eddy went way back in their criminal careers - they had been closely tied for about a decade now. Tommy would be furious if he is tied to this crime, for any reason. Third, since he royally fucked up the burglary in the magnificent Oyster Bay house, Tommy probably will not bail him out - if bail is even offered.

Eddy had a pretty extensive rap sheet on file and the judge may not offer bail this time. His other arrests included Criminal Possession

Weapon, Menacing, Assault, Resisting Arrest, and Criminal Mischief, but they had never lead to prison time. The thought of being holed up in some crappy prison for any length of time put Eddy on edge.

He cannot serve time again! The first and only prison sentence was for seven years for Armed Robbery and Eddy thought he would lose his mind in that place. The brutal treatment he endured as a virgin inmate was beyond imagination. He was raped and beaten almost daily for a year until another inmate took care of him - for services rendered, of course.

Eddy hated it, but it was better to take care of old Harry's needs than to be at the mercy of everyone else. Plus, Harry did not expect it every day. When these cops, Sargent Anthony Craven and Officer Michael Sorren first arrested him, they searched him thoroughly - or so they thought. Eddy knew a trick or two and he was always prepared for another arrest when he was working a job.

The two cops from Oyster Bay were elated that they successfully captured such an outstanding career criminal. So elated, that one could almost hear them crowing as they related all the details to their superior back at headquarters. Once all the paperwork was completed and confirmed with the New York Police Department, it was decided that they would transport Eddy to Manhattan where he would be held pending arraignment on the next business day.

Now it was time to transport Eddy to the city police department where a judge would handle his case. Suddenly, he was not feeling too well, and Eddy requested to use the bathroom before they put him in the squad car. He did need the use of a bathroom, but only because he wanted to retrieve the tiny, homemade shiv, that was stored inside his anus.

AT A MOMENT'S NOTICE

That shiv was the size of his thumb but big enough to do plenty of damage if handled properly. It was housed inside a homemade container made of a waterproof, plastic toothpick holder and shoved up inside his rectum anytime he went out on a job. *Ah yes,* Eddy chuckled to himself, *just one of the many educational benefits of our prison system. This is one trick I learned well and have used many times.*

Eddy had the tiny shiv carefully hidden away, tucked underneath the lapel of his jailhouse jumpsuit and readily accessible at a moment's notice. The officer's had no idea, and failed to search him again. The two officers placed Eddy into the back seat of their patrol car and proceeded to make the long drive to Manhattan, intending to hand their prisoner over for tomorrow's arraignment.

About thirty minutes into the drive, Eddy began to squirm around in the backseat, and once again asked to use the restroom, "Sorry guys, I got a problem. I need the bathroom again. Sargent Craven locates a gas station they can use. They pull over and uncuff him once they are outside the bathroom.

Suddenly, Eddy swings around with his shiv, slashing the closest officer and getting him right in the carotid artery! Officer Sorren steps back in surprise, screaming and holding his throat to stem the tremendous flow of blood. Blood was squirting everywhere, and Michael Sorren did not have a chance; he died within a minute of being slashed.

Eddy quickly went after Sargent Craven next but the experienced officer already had his gun drawn and was firing rapidly, each bullet finding its mark in Fast Eddy! Eddy died with a surprised look on his face. Eddy fell to the floor, with blood gurgling out of several bullet wounds. His last words were: "You bastard!"

Sargent Craven was extremely shaken, breathing heavily, leaning against the wall and trembling visibly. "Oh my God, oh my God, what have I done?" hollers Sargent Craven. "Mike! Oh, dear God! Mike!" The gas station clerk nervously peeked around the corner. "You ok, officer?" she asks. "Call an ambulance, and the local police!" yells Sargent Craven as he kneels over the fallen officer. "Mike, I am so sorry", he whispers as he places his own jacket over his partner and friend.

CHAPTER THIRTY-ONE

Case Closed

Chief Walter Hadley is at his wit's end over the unsolved murders of the Pratels. It is now two weeks after their murder, and his investigators have exhausted their leads. During the early morning meeting, Walter and his investigating team spent four hours examining every notation, as well as every aspect of each document they had accrued on the case.

No discrepancies showed up, no errors were found - the case was mindboggling. He was very disturbed that all leads became dead ends. There was only one hope left: The small, private police department of the exclusive town of Oyster Bay, Long Island, arrested a burglar last night who had a stellar criminal rap sheet.

That prisoner was being brought in today to answer for open bench warrants. He was also to be questioned with regard to the Pratel murders based on his criminal records. Fast Eddy Capatelli made the perfect suspect to this case, but hard evidence was needed and that is what he was hoping to receive today.

During the prisoner's questioning in Oyster Bay, some interesting facts had come to light; Walter wanted and needed that information.

Around noon, Walter received a phone call from the Oyster Bay Police Department - the prisoner had been killed during an attempted escape while being transported to Manhattan!

Walter put his caller on hold and sat back with a stunned look on his face. He felt a cold sweat break out on his body and he could barely breathe. His suspect had been killed! He could not question him now. "No! I do not believe this crap! Was the prisoner taken out, or was it an accident?" *Why can't I get a break on this case,* he thought to himself. Picking up the phone again, Chief Hadley orders that police officer to report in to his Manhattan office, bringing whatever paperwork and evidence he had.

He lost the opportunity to question the criminal, but he can still get that vital information from the arresting officer. *What else can go wrong?* Walter thinks in despair. Sargent Craven arrives at the precinct at one o'clock PM and sits down with Chief Hadly and the chief investigator, David Sperl.

Two hours are spent carefully going over the considerable evidence and documentation delivered by Anthony Craven. Finally, Walter looks up and says, "Sargent, this is decent evidence when combined with the evidence we have. The two sets of evidence complement each other, forging links that we did not have before.

You interviewed him thoroughly and documented with clarity. I can go to the judge with this; let me show you how it all fits together." Walter goes to the chalkboard in the station's briefing room and quickly sketches a diagram that depicts how everything combined shows a clear picture of how Fast Eddy may have been the killer in the Pratel murders.

The proof is not one hundred percent, but it is close enough for a jury to rule against Fast Eddy in the courtroom, if they had gone to trial. *It is damn close,* Walter thinks with elation. "Ok guys, we are done here for today. Sargent, I will see that you get copies of everything for your records, but I will need the originals for the judge. Thanks for coming right in, I will send a pay voucher over to Chief Lane in Oyster Bay for your compensation."

Walter turns to his clerical assistant, "Sharon, find out when Judge Johansen is available for a meeting, he needs to see this evidence and I will present it myself." "Yes sir," answers Sharon. At five o'clock that afternoon, Chief Hadley presents his convincing evidence to Judge Johansen and they go over it together for about thirty minutes.

The judge agrees that the evidence is conclusive, and decides to formally close the case of the Pratel murders. Walter is grinning when he leaves the judge's chambers. *Solved! The case is solved!* Chief Hadley cannot wait to tell the mayor, but first he needs to pull back all the subsidiary searches that are still in progress.

He ordered searches several days ago, not only for the suspect, but also for that witness that went missing. There is no need to waste manpower on that when the case has been closed. Although it came in a roundabout way, Fast Eddy was posthumously charged with the murder of the Pratels in Manhattan on March 6, 1957.

In reality, Angelo Comino was the murderer whom Tommy Two Toes had sent to deliver that blow. But Chief Hadly is reasonably sure that Fast Eddy Capatelli was the murderer and he was quite relieved that the case is officially closed. Suddenly, a very sad thought entered his mind – I will have to call that wife in Long Island to tell her we could not find her husband.

CHAPTER THIRTY-TWO

No Resistance

Jonathan slept soundly for many hours while the truck driver continued on his route to Montana. The driver was still wondering just what he had gotten himself into, picking up this stranger. He was concerned about his passenger after hearing about the manhunt for a dangerous murderer - was this guy that murderer?

Well, he will know soon enough. They will be coming to the North Dakota/Minnesota border in about an hour, where all vehicles were being thoroughly searched. Meanwhile, the patrol units stationed at the state border were just given orders to break off the search. It is over - the murderer was found in New York City and the case was closed.

The troop of officers pulled out and returned to their regular duties, disappointed that they were not going to be a part of this infamous manhunt after all. The case had made all the papers from coast to coast, and it had been exciting news. About thirty minutes later, the trucker suddenly noticed the uniformed troops passing him on the opposite side of the interstate.

Those must be the guys from the border stop, he thought. *If they are disbanding, they must have caught their man. Sure glad it was not my hitch hiker.* He breathes a sigh of relief just as Jonathan finally opens his eyes. With a liberating stretch, Jonathan addresses his driver. "Hey there, I slept like a dead man! It was just what I needed. Will we be stopping anytime soon? I sure could use the bathroom - and a fresh cup of Joe!"

"Sure!" responds the trucker. "There is a good truck stop coming up in a couple of miles. We will go in together and get a meal while we are in there. We should plan on staying the night; there are too many miles before we come across another decent truck stop and it is way too far to continue on to Boseman tonight.

We can bunk down right here in the cab of the truck. There is plenty of room for us both." "Sounds good to me", replies Jonathan, but his mind is on Viola. He longs to see his old friend and is glad he decided to alter his life in this direction. She will give him time and space to think clearly to get his life together again.

Viola's not the type of broad to smother a guy, the way that Susan always did. Susan is a good wife, but she had a habit of clinging too tightly. A man needs his own breathing room! *The kids are a lot of fun and he will miss them,* Jon thinks. *Well, they will adjust to life without their Dad after some time passes. It is better this way,* he reasons.

I cannot see putting them in danger from the mob, and I cannot move around freely with children to worry about. Susan will take good care of them; she's a good mother. Jonathan had no idea of the huge manhunt that was just discontinued, and the danger he had been in from the police.

He also had no idea of the current status of Tommy Two Toes, but he assumed that he was still being hunted by those gangsters and the local NYC police. Right now, he is focused on getting to California safely, without any more interference from the police. Two hours later, the men were relaxing with a smoke and a drink, sharing the local newspaper and chatting over current events.

"Will ya look-it this", says the driver who introduced himself as Stan. "There has been a big search for some murderer from NYC, even way out here." As he spoke those words he was carefully watching Jonathan. Jonathan spoke up brightly, saying, "Yes I know about that. People say he killed a pastor and his wife in the city. Who would want to shoot down a pastor? What is the world coming to?

There is too much crime in that city. Instead of New York City, it should be called True Crime City." Stan was instantly at ease, feeling much better about his rider. There was no guilty sense about Jonathan at all. "C'mon, it is getting late. We have an early start if I am gonna make Boseman on schedule tomorrow."

They got settled into Stan's bunkhouse for the night, and Jonathan laid there for a long while, wide awake and thinking of his next few steps. He will find Viola in California - he knows she will be living in the same place. He knew that Viola is not one to move around a lot. He will need to find someone to make him a new identity with papers and a story to match, and then he will start looking for work.

It would be great if he could find work as a mechanic - he was always good at fixing things. Jon loved to tinker with gadgets of all kinds. Maybe he will even set up his own little part time shop. *Yeah! Smarty's Fix It Shop! Uh huh.* He would be keeping close tabs on the gangsters for a long while, but perhaps they would not come this far west. If they come to bother him out here, he will have to run again. *I hope it does not come to that.* Those are his last thoughts before drifting off to sleep for the night.

CHAPTER THIRTY-THREE

Richard Bandeau Returns to NYC

When Chief Hadley learned who Fast Eddy Capatelli worked for, he knew for certain that Tommy Two Toes was the man responsible for ordering the death of the Pratels. He also knew exactly where Tommy lived. He had known for a long time and was just waiting for the right opportunity to grab the gangster who had sent so many people to an early grave. Finally, that opportunity arrived.

The Chief picked up his phone and called Detective Carlson. "I want you and Bentworth to take a backup team over to Tommy Two Toes' apartment. Arrest the son of a bitch for the death of the Pratels and bring him back here - throw him in the lockup!" He heard Carlson mumble something incoherently and it only infuriated him further.

"I do not care that there is no search warrant! I have enough cause to pick him up and I want you guys over there now! You do not have to go inside - figure out how to get him out of the apartment! Go!" An hour later, the two detectives have figured out that Tommy was not home.

They still had no idea of the horrors that were within those walls, and when they found out later, they would both become violently ill. For now, the fate of Lucinda remained a silent mystery. The team of policemen began canvassing the neighborhood, covering a four square block area. They are looking for Tommy Two Toes; or for anyone with any knowledge of where he may have gone.

As the neighborhood is canvassed, one neighbor, a scruffy old guy with a limp, comes forward. "I saw them leave - Tommy Two Toes, that big hoodlum, and his sidekick. They left a little over an hour ago. I know the young guy - he lives a dozen blocks away on East Third. Drives a Thunderbird. I saw them get in it and drive off in that direction."

Det. Carlson realized this witness had provided critically important information about the location. He asks, " What is your name? Do you live around here? Is there anything else you can tell me?" "Oh, I am Charlie Bean and I live right on that corner there. Got a great view of both sides of the street from apartment number five.

I am home most times since I lost my job a few years ago. I have nothin' to do 'cept watch the neighbors. You kin call on me anytime, Detective", he said with a grin. "I like being part of all the excitement. Don't have no phone though; you'll have ta come around." Carlson made notes in his book while Charlie was talking.

As the elderly neighbor turned away to leave, he suddenly turned back and added a comment, "Hope you get them guys. They a real bad bunch. Always noisy, causing a ruckus. Ya should have heard the noise up there this morning. That lady screamed blue-bloody murder. I never heard such noise!"

When the conversation ended, he hollered, "Let's go Bentworth! Bring the team; we are going to look for that T-Bird a few blocks from here on East Third. That is where we will find Tommy." Meanwhile, Officer Bandeau finally returned to Manhattan the afternoon that Tommy was being tracked down.

He returned to his department, and to a very angry Chief Hadley. Oh! Did he ever reap the whirlwind! Chief Hadley was really mad at him, and Richard was disciplined harshly for taking off on his own, instead of working alongside the rest of the department. Richard Bandeau originally thought he could solve the case himself.

He was so sure that Jonathan had been the murderer - after all, an innocent man does not run and hide. The entire squad knew that Jonathan had witnessed the murders, but Richard was absolutely convinced that Jonathan *was* the murderer. His thinking was based on Jonathan's behavior, on his taking off and leaving his family behind, with no word.

He actually caught the missing witness, but was outsmarted by Jonathan and had to return home empty-handed. He was mortified. Not only was it a humiliation, but his boss unloaded his wrath upon him in the form of punishment. Richard was now suspended without pay for the next four months. "It is going to be a very long four months," thought Richard with a heavy heart, as he turned in his badge and his gun.

CHAPTER THIRTY-FOUR

We're Going Home!

The Patelli's have spent the past week at the hideaway mountain cabin, enjoying the serene surroundings, in spite of their anxiety over current circumstances. At the moment, the two children are playing in the basement, and the parents are in the living room with Sargent Whitfield, who is currently on duty.

"I just wish we were done with this", Carolyn says to Sam. "You should be back to work, the children need to be in school, and I want my normal life back" she laments to her husband, who knew the stress was building each day that nothing happened, and was driving her crazy.

Sam takes her in his arms and hugs her tightly. "Just a little while longer", he says in a soothing voice. "It will be over soon, I promise." Suddenly, there is shouting from the basement. Sam goes to the doorway and hollers down to the kids, "Hey! What is going on?" Tommy replies with a whine, "She took my fire truck and will not give it back!"

Wanda starts yelling back at Tommy, "I will give it back when you stop pestering me for every little thing." She mimics Tommy with his complaints in a high-pitched voice, "When are we going home? When are we going to eat? I am hungry! I am tired of this place."

Wanda looks at her little brother, Tommy, right in the eyes and says, "We will go home when Mommy and Daddy say we can, and not a minute sooner. Got that, pip-squeak? Now shut up!" Sam looks at Carolyn, shaking his head. "They are tired of being cooped up in here."

At that moment, the phone rings and Sargent Whitfield answers it. "Whitfield" he says. Then he listens intently for several minutes. "Yes sir, I understand", he replies. Hanging up, Benny is all smiles.

"We are going home, folks!" he yells. Benny gets up and walks over to the basement door. "Wanda! Tommy! C'mon up here, kids!" The astonished parents look at him in total surprise. "Really?" says Carolyn. "We can go home? What happened? Is it over?" Sam just stood there, speechless.

Wanda and Tommy have joined them in the living room and are rattling off questions simultaneously. "Can't we stay another week?" whines Wanda. "Mom, I do not wanna go back to school!" Tommy is shouting, "Yeah! Just wait 'til I tell the gang back home that we had a super vacation involving police action and everything! I can tell Harry and David and Billy - can't I Mom?"

"Ok, kids. Settle down now and go pack your things." says Carolyn. Be sure to double check that you do not leave anything behind!" With that, she turns to Benny and requests more information. She looks at Sgt. Whitfield expectantly; "look, be square with us now. What is going on?"

"Just a moment, let me get my partner so I only have to say this once." Benny goes to wake up Henry, who was fast asleep, waiting for his shift to begin. The two officers return in a couple of minutes with mugs of coffee and sit down with the Patelli's. "It is over," explains Sargent Whitfield. "The murderer was apprehended in Oyster Bay and killed while attempting to escape."

"What about the mob? Won't another thug be sent in his place?" asks Sam. "Are you sure no one else is coming after us?" Clearly, Sam is worried about going home. "I just got word from Chief Hadley," explains Benny. "The murderer was killed while attempting escape, and his boss is a well-known mobster from Manhattan.

A team of officers is rounding them up as we speak. By the time we get back to Manhattan - remember, it is a six hour drive - the entire deal will be wrapped up." Carolyn and Sam just looked at each other in silence. Could it be true? Was their exile from home and relatives finally over?

It seemed to take forever, but now they could go home to resume their family life again. Would it be the same, or would it be altered forever? Sam gazes longingly at Carolyn. "I love you and the kids. I am so sorry I put us all in danger! I just wanted to do the right thing. Never again! I will never do something like that again without examining all the potential consequences."

"Oh, Sam," replies Carolyn. "I know you did not intend any harm. We will be okay, but we might need some time to relax and let our raw emotions heal. Life will get back to normal, you will see." With that, she embraced her husband and just held on tight for a few moments. As she let go of their embrace, "C'mon Sam, let's get packed. We are going home!" Sam had not seen her smile like that for a long while.

CHAPTER THIRTY-FIVE

Who is Missing?

When Gary and Tommy got to his apartment, Gary spent several minutes getting Tommy settled down before breaking away to make a discreet phone call. That call was made to a well-trusted cleanup man whom Tommy had used for many occasions such as this; a man who cleans up any messy business left behind by Tommy's hoods so there would be no traces left for the police to follow.

He is only known by the name of Angus, and his location has never been discovered because he has always lived constantly on the move. Once a job was performed, Angus would move his living quarters, staying two steps ahead of the police at all times.

Gary understood that Tommy would never be able to return to his headquarters and he gave Angus instructions to completely demolish Tommy's apartment, office, garage, torture chamber in the basement, and the Cadillac. There was to be nothing left.

Not only were the police after Tommy, but also the gang who killed Lucinda and ruined the new Cadillac. It was Gary's hope that this would put a stop to any kind of investigation or trace of their whereabouts. He then returned to Tommy's side to check on him. Gary found him still in a state of shock, mumbling incoherently and nursing his stiff drink of whiskey.

Angus immediately took his cleanup toolkit and went to the address where Tommy lived, only to find the place crawling with cops. They did not appear to be inside the dwelling yet, but the entire neighborhood was being canvassed by officers. Questions were being asked, answers were being noted, and it was too late for him to do his job.

How did they get here so fast? Angus wondered as he immediately left the vicinity. He was not about to get caught up in that mess. He would need to relocate anyway since he was seen driving through the area. Returning to his office, Angus called Gary back with the bad news. "It was too late to do anything and you two should get out while you can," Angus told Gary. "Just leave right this minute and you might have a chance."

Suddenly there was a loud *bang!* and Gary dropped the phone to run into the next room. Tommy found one of Gary's revolvers hidden in a side drawer and blew his brains out by putting it in his mouth and pulling the trigger. The entire top of his head was gone, splattered against the living room wall, with the gun still loosely held in his hand.

Hanging his head in sadness, Gary's tears are flowing down his cheeks. Tommy was a real bastard at times but, he did not deserve to end his life in this manner. Gary thinks about the tightly-knit group. Fast Eddy's whereabouts are unknown, presumably dead or caught by the police.

Now Lucinda and Tommy Two Toes are dead. The entire organization is unraveling quickly and Gary is certain the police are en route to his apartment. With no time to mourn, he throws his cash, weapons and identification into a bag and runs out of there.

Gary leaves his Thunderbird behind – it is too conspicuous - and takes off for the nearest subway train. He will ride the rails for a while until he can think of a good plan.

Meanwhile, four officers are sent to search Gary's apartment and the other policemen have received permission from Chief Hadley to enter Tommy's residence.

They are a hardy bunch who have seen most everything, but the carnage inside Tommy's apartment stuns them into absolute silence. The officers cannot believe the bloody mess left by Lucinda's grisly death. The entire block is cordoned off while waiting for the Police Photographer and the Coroner to arrive, and the team of officers continue their search of the premises.

They quickly look through the entire residence beyond the living room and kitchen. The offices are found and will be searched in detail a bit later, and the garage yields no clues other than the damaged Cadillac. When the basement is discovered, every officer begins speaking at once.

Never in their long careers have they seen such a torture chamber. It is as if they stepped onto a movie set with devices of every imaginable horror. They could not help themselves; they felt compelled to examine each piece in wonder and curiosity. The forensics team would have a field day with this!

Upon arrival at Gary's place, that team of police find the door unlocked and walk into another bloody scene - Tommy's bloody death. Was it murder or suicide? The youngest officer turns to his partner and says, "These guys were ruthless killers, but I wonder if we got them all. Who else should we be looking for? Whose apartment is this? Who is Tommy's right-hand man, and where is he?"

CHAPTER THIRTY-SIX

Jennifer's Next Step

Susan was relieved when her daughter, Jennifer, returned home that night just before dinnertime. She was both furious and tearful at the same time, telling him, "Jennifer, after dinner you will do the dishes tonight and then we are going to have a talk. Is that clear?" "Yes, Mom," Jennifer replied, as Susan picked up the phone to notify the police department.

Jennifer knew there would be trouble when she returned home. She just did not know what *kind* of trouble. While she was on the phone with the police, she was informed that Bill, the man arrested at her home earlier, would not be bothering her again.

Bill turned out to be quite a thief and was being incarcerated for grand larceny - everything from jewelry to vehicles. He was wanted in several counties across New York State. Jennifer was being groomed by Bill as an accomplice because of her youth and apparent innocence.

The police were not pressing any charges against Jennifer, but they sternly warned Susan that the next occurrence could result in a permanent record against the girl. The dinner hour was lively with conversation between Michelle, Amanda and Todd, leaving Susan time to mentally prepare her comments for Jennifer.

Mostly they were chatting about Todd's workday, which gave a pleasant atmosphere to the evening. Todd was engaging the kids in 'what if' scenarios, a game they often played. It went a long way towards helping everyone to relax. When Jennifer was finished cleaning up the dinner dishes, she sat by her mother who was waiting in the living room. The time was around 6:30. With a sigh, Susan said, "Ok, go to your room and we will speak there. I will be right up."

Again, Jennifer replied, "Yes, Mom." A couple of minutes after Jennifer went to her room expecting the worst, Susan knocked on her door before entering. She stood there looking at her for a full minute before speaking to her. The extended silence made Jennifer feel extremely uncomfortable. She knew she was in a lot of hot water and did not know what would happen next.

"I have had it with you," Susan begins. "You are making life even harder for everyone in this household, and I am not going to take it anymore." "Mom, I..." Jennifer begins, but Susan cuts her off harshly. "I do not even want to hear your excuses," she says.

I have had it, and you are not going to stay here for a while. I have made arrangements for you to attend the school for troubled youths in Glen Cove, NY. They are picking you up at 8:00 PM tonight, so pack a bag. Only one suitcase is allowed, so make smart choices."

"But, Mom..." Jennifer tries again to reason with her angry mother. The look she cast on her at that moment was the meanest, angriest look she had ever seen from her, and she snapped her mouth shut. "As I said, you are not going to live here anymore, and that school will provide strict discipline.

You will have to grow up and become an honest, hardworking student, or you will fail miserably and there will be no one to bail you out of trouble. I will not come to your rescue." Susan took another breath and said, "I love you dearly, and that is the only reason I am willing to do this. I am not giving up on you - don't you give up on you, either."

With that said, Susan walked out of her room. That evening, a smartly dressed school official arrived to pick up Jennifer and her one suitcase. After a brief hug, Susan let her go, not letting her see her tears. She could not afford the expense of a private school, but for her sake, she could not afford *not* to send her.

Todd witnessed this action and stopped in a little later to ask her if she needed to talk. "No," she replied tersely, and she went to check on her other two daughters. She did not want Todd to become too deeply immersed in her personal family affairs. Amanda was already in bed and Michelle was finishing her homework. "How is school, honey?" Susan asks.

"Great, Mom. I love my teachers this year. I will not be any trouble," replies Michelle tentatively. "Do not worry, sweetie. You are never a problem. Jennifer needed to go away so she could be around strong counselors - leaders who could teach her strong values. Do you understand?" "Yes, I think so. You are not teaching her a lesson. You are doing something good for her," Michelle responds. "Will you miss her?" Susan sighs, "I already do."

CHAPTER THIRTY-SEVEN

Viola

Early in the morning, Stan and Jonathan get on the road again after getting a supply of fresh coffee and sticky buns to take along. As they continue to chat, Jonathan asked his driver if he might be able to hitch a ride from another driver that is going to California.

"Sure," says Stan. "Once we reach Boseman I will put the word out for you. It is always good to have a passenger to help keep you awake, and I will let them know that you are a standup kinda guy. It should not be a problem to get a ride right from where I am making my delivery."

"Great!" Jonathan continues to chat with Stan, and now they are talking about those murders in NYC again. It is still front page news, now that the police found their man. Jonathan continues to be wide-eyed innocent about the whole affair, but he keeps trying to change the subject.

Finally he is able to get Stan talking about his own little family living in the suburbs of Chattanooga, Tennessee. He is happy to tell his tales about Katie Sue and his three boys, Brady, Billy and Bobby for the rest of the trip. They arrive in Boseman and Stan finds a ride for

Jonathan with another driver going to Southern California. The two men shake hands and wish each other well, and Jonathan goes off with a man named Charlie.

It takes them two days of driving before they reach their destination of Bakersfield, CA. Jonathan remembered that Buena Vista is just a couple of hours south of Bakersfield on Route 5. He thanks Charlie for the ride and continues on his way, hitching another ride going south. The trip has been uneventful although long, but he is almost there.

Once he is in Buena Vista, Jonathan makes his first stop at a second-hand clothing store. There is not much money in his wallet, but he buys a pair of jeans, two t-shirts and some fresh underwear for a few days. Jonathan checks into a cheap motel so he can grab a hot shower, a quick meal and some rest. The next day he will stop in to see his lovely Viola.

Jonathan rises with the sun. He showers and puts on clean clothes, then heads out to the last known address for Viola. He hoped and prayed she would still be living there.

"Ok," he says to himself. "This is the place she bought long ago. Wow, it is really looking nice now. She has been working hard on the gardens - the yard is beautiful!" When she moved in about fifteen years ago the gardens were nothing but sand and dried weeds. *Well, here goes,* he thinks as he rings the bell at the side door.

Viola comes to the door and she looked through the screen. It took her a long moment to recognize him. Then she throws the door open, welcoming Jonathan immediately. "Jonny! I just knew you would be out to find me again when I heard all the bad news on the television. Come in!"

Jonathan enters and throws his arms around his west coast sweetheart. "Viola, I have really missed you! I should have stayed out here with you. Will you forgive me?" "Oh, you!" She exclaims. "Come, we will have breakfast together and we will talk. I have to hear about everything!" She says as she makes fresh coffee, sets the table for two and begins preparing breakfast. He sat down and his mouth was watering as she prepared their meal.

After breakfast they each get another cup of coffee and begin catching up on what Viola has been doing. She has a good job as a kindergarten school teacher and in her spare time she works in the gardens. Hot days are spent playing the piano - she has become quite accomplished and puts on a summer concert in the local park each year. She loves to perform in front of an audience and the entire town turns out for her charity events. All proceeds from the concert tickets are donated to her favorite local church. "But what about you, Jonathan? Didn't you get married? What happened to your family? Where do you stand with the law? Are they looking for you? The news reports say that they got their criminal. What about the mob? Are they still looking for you as well?"

Jonathan explains to Viola that the killer has been found and he is off the hook with the law; no one should be looking for him. He has no intention of returning to Susan, and will simply vanish from that life. He will miss the kids, but they will be better off without him. Susan will take good care of them; she is a lot tougher than he is as a parent.

Viola takes his hands into hers and looks at him intently. "Jonathan, I have a great life here. It took a long time to build my life. You can stay here if you are completely free of any east coast mess. You have to find out before we settle together, Jonathan." With that said, Viola leaves the table to clean up her kitchen. Jonathan is left alone in the room, drinking his coffee and wondering what he will do next.

Epilogue: One Year Later

It is amazing how many lives were changed at a moment's notice, just because one man witnessed a crime that took place in Manhattan that night in March, 1957. Susan, Michelle, Amanda and Todd settled into a daily routine that created an atmosphere of stability.

The children have come to accept Todd and have come to understand that he is here to stay. Although it is still a mystery why, they know that Daddy is not coming back. They miss their Daddy so much, especially Michelle, who has such vivid memories of time spent with her father. For Amanda, the memories of her father are becoming very faint because she is so young.

Jennifer has proven to be an excellent student at the academy in Glen Cove. She buckled down and became a straight-A student after many episodes of misbehavior that resulted in severe discipline. She actually thanked her mother for sending her to such a strict private school.

She knows that she could not afford to send her there, but made a sacrifice to do it out of her love for her. Although they live apart, Jennifer's appreciation for her family has grown immeasurably. She looks forward to spending her summer and holiday vacations with them.

Susan continues to spend time trying to find her husband, and is saving money to hire a private investigator to help find him. The local police have moved on to more recent cases since the thirteen state APB investigation turned up no clues or leads. Even Chief Hadley could not hold out any hope for Susan when he came to the house to tell her in person that the search was called off and the case was closed because the murderer was found.

There does not seem to be any more traces of Jonathan, and that leaves Susan wondering if she will ever know the truth of what happened to her husband. The Patelli family resumed their normal lifestyle without fear of repercussion. It took about six months before they felt comfortable and safe again, as it was clear that no one was looking for them anymore.

Tommy and Wanda still have nightmares about their experience. Young Wanda asked one night, "All the bad guys are gone now, right, Mommy?" The parents will always remember the terror they went through. The Pratel family are still grieving their beloved Shelby and Candi, not finding any peace in the knowledge that the men responsible for their murders died horrible deaths. They just feel a deep, painful grief that is endured silently each day as they live out their lives.

Jonathan and Viola have become the closest of friends and lovers again, enjoying each other's company. Jonathan has opened his own handyman shop in the barn behind Viola's garage. It is called "Smarty's Fix-it Shop" and he repairs small appliances such as toasters, lamps and irons, even lawnmowers and the occasional television. He loves the work he is doing and has already built up a profitable and loyal clientele.

While he is busy tinkering in his shop, Viola works in her gardens. She loves nothing more than to play in the dirt and make everything in her yard bloom. On hot, summer days she plays her piano for hours on end, with Jonathan and the occasional male neighbor as her audience. The two men often play a few hands of poker while she plays. Viola still performs her concerts in the summer, and most of the townspeople turn out to enjoy her music.

Jonathan might always have to be on the lookout for gangsters or police investigators, in spite of the case being closed. To keep his true identity under wraps and to appease Viola, he had his name legally changed to James Alexander. He found it easy to get a new social security number, simply by filing an application.

His friends call him Al. So far he had not entertained any thoughts of cheating on Viola - he was not taking any chances on ruining the new life he was enjoying. Al was hopeful that he and Viola would have many peaceful years together. Gary Caputo, the right hand man for Tommy at the end of his life, moved on to Chicago to join the mob out there. He thought it wise to get out of New York in case the police were still looking for him.

The mob boss in Chicago was impressed with both Gary's skills and character. He handled himself well and has shown himself to be an accurate judge of people and situations. There was even talk of Gary being given a district of his own to govern, as a test.

He has a promising career in his chosen path of ruthless crime and continues to hone his skills. Gary's dream is to become a high-priced professional mercenary, an assassin for hire, working independently of any Mob boss. "That is the end of the story," Amanda tells the group at Carmine's.

"Now you know the sad truth of what happened to our father. Mom did not get the painful facts from that private investigator until just a short time ago, forty years later, when he stumbled upon

Jonathan, who was now known as Al, while looking for someone else. The investigator remembered the case from decades ago because it was so unique.

Mom was glad to finally learn the truth about what happened and have closure before her own death. She told me the entire story just a couple of weeks ago, as she knew her time was near."

As the family heard the unbelievable truth of what happened to their father long ago, a loud buzz of cross-conversations began all at once.

Amanda looked around the room and studied the various looks of surprise, shock and disbelief. It would take some time for the story to sink in, but now the truth was known and their mom could rest in peace.

About the Author

Author of "At a Moment's Notice", Carole grew up in South Huntington, NY. After she married in 1975 she moved to Deltona, Florida with her husband.

Carole became divorced and moved to Central Florida, where she remained until returning to New York when her mother began to experience some mild health issues. She returned home in 1994 to assist her mother who was living alone.

Carole always loved to write but didn't begin to publish her work until 2013. Her first book was a caregiver resource guide, "There's No One Like Mom", which focuses on critical caregiving needs for the elderly. The book is highlighted with amusing true stories of her life while caring for her aging mother.

This second book, "At a Moment's Notice", is a fast paced suspense novel that keeps the reader on edge until the final page. Although this is a work of fiction, segments of the story are excerpted from the author's own family history.

www.ingramcontent.com/pod-product-compliance
Lightning Source LLC
LaVergne TN
LVHW041846070526
838199LV00045BA/1460